Copyright © 2025 John Sidebottom All rights reserved

The characters and events portrayed in this book are fictitious. Any similarity to real persons, living or dead, is coincidental and not intended by the author.

No part of this book may be reproduced, or stored in a retrieval system, or transmitted in any form or by any means, electronic, mechanical, photocopying, recording, or otherwise, without the express written permission of the publisher.

Prologue

Cambridge in October smelled of wet stone and bicycle oil — but the air reeked of secrets. Traded in whispers, filed in archives, sometimes weaponised.

Lanes narrowed without warning, funnelling students through a city older than most nations. Damp air from the Cam soaked the stone, carrying the must of ink and paper from the library, fryer smoke clinging to the market square, the tang of coal smoke after rain. Posters for a Poll Tax protest sagged on the railings.

In the restricted archives, Simon Arkwright found a brown folder stamped with a fading Ministry crest. Inside: references to "non-standard consumables" and "dual-use tooling" bound for the Middle East before the Gulf War (Ref: DTI/EXP/90/NS-12). Euphemisms sharpened to slip past the untrained eye. One line — "tooling for turbine assemblies" — told him it wasn't just noise.

Julian barely looked up when Simon mentioned it. His cufflinks sat uneven. A hand trembled before he let it fall flat against the desk — a crack in the armour, small but real. Simon noticed. Nerves? Illness? Or an old wound surfacing in the quiet?

Julian had spoken before of mentors, men who promised opportunity but left shadows behind. Simon had thought it was bravado. Now he wasn't sure.

"Old bureaucratic noise, Simon. The world runs on it." Footsteps in the corridor: measured, unhurried, too close.

―――

Simon walked through Cambridge as if it were already mapped in his head. Cloisters and cobblestones weren't heritage — they were systems to break. At the Union bar, he couldn't help noticing the till: flimsy lock, one screw already loose. He filed it away without thinking.

Across the room, Sophie Patel watched him. While others filled the air with noise, she listened. Sharp eyes.

Sharper questions. The kind that unsettled even when she smiled. She slid a half-empty glass across the table into his reach without asking, then tilted her head.

"You don't strike me as someone who likes rules," she said, almost idly. But the way she held his gaze made it clear it wasn't a question.

He told himself she was just another student. He knew better.

Julian's voice cut like glass.

"One week Iraq's the enemy, the next they're partners. That isn't reality. It's theatre. Brussels writes unity; the headlines sell division. Stories are leashes."

He had arrived the same week but looked born for the place: tailored coat, precise diction, scanning rooms as if they already belonged to him. Cutlery scraped. Conversations dipped, then rose again.

Simon's answer was simple.

"Yes."

Julian's was slower.

"Only if it leads somewhere worth going."

Neither of them knew how many locked doors lay ahead — or that three years later, one of them would stand on a misted Cambridgeshire farm road, staring at a white panel van idling too quietly.

———

Somewhere, a hinge groaned. A door closed. The story had already begun.

Chapter 1

The first thing Simon Arkwright noticed about Cambridge wasn't the spires.

It was the locks.

Even in the fog, the city's defences stood out to him. Mill Road smelled of chip fat and damp coal dust, undercut by the faint ozone hum of overhead lines. Everywhere he walked, his mind catalogued barriers: medieval bolts polished by centuries of hands, Yale cylinders on stairwell doors, the battered pigeonhole cabinet in the porter's lodge that would yield to a screwdriver. Obstacles to most. Invitations to him.

He'd cut his teeth on a ZX Spectrum and a clattering Amstrad, dialling into bulletin boards long before most kids had heard the word modem. FidoNet squeals, green-screen commands, the hiss of a phone line hijacked for a midnight connection — that was his apprenticeship.

At thirteen, it had been the chemistry storeroom. A padlock so old it felt like a dare. Inside: jars of formaldehyde, copper sulphate, and his cousin's name scrawled on the register instead of his. A week later, the cousin took the blame. Simon could have spoken. He didn't. In Belfast kitchens thick with smoke, he had already learned that silence was survival. Rules weren't guidance. They were errors waiting to be corrected.

By day two in Cambridge, he had mapped the college's master-key system. By the end of the week, he'd slipped into the computer lab after hours and gained root access. Not to cause trouble. Only to prove it was possible — and to leave himself a hidden door no one else could see.

Julian Thorne first spoke to him in a panelled room above the Old Library. Chalk dust and radiator heat thickened the air. A trace of aftershave lingered — sharp, cheap, era-worn Brut — as if someone else had just left. Rain pattered against the leaded glass.

Julian answered a question on council spending with the ease of someone used to being listened to. Politics bled into every discussion after Thatcher's fall, and he wielded it like a scalpel — aligning a stray spoon before he spoke, as if even the room required correction. He spoke like men twice his age, the kind who offered patronage with one hand and ownership with the other.

Simon moved to leave. Julian was already in the doorway.

"You broke into the lab server last week." Not a question.

Simon said nothing, the way he had as a boy when silence was safer than truth.

"You didn't change anything," Julian went on. "Didn't even touch your own permissions. You only wanted to see if you could."

"That was the point," Simon said.

Julian studied him, then smiled — not warmth, but recognition.

"Then you understand. You and I should talk."

His questions came like chess moves, traps already set. Simon learned Julian studied philosophy, politics, and economics — a course for those who intended to run things. Julian learned Simon's relationship with locks, digital or physical, was compulsion, not rebellion. His question was always the same: who locked this, and why?

When they stepped into the night, the rain had cleared. Streetlamps glowed amber. Shopfront glass threw their silhouettes back at them. Julian walked with hands in pockets, glancing sideways as if he had just acquired something valuable.

Simon couldn't tell if he'd made a friend — or just stepped onto a board he'd never leave.

Chapter 2

The computer lab was never quiet. Fans hummed, fluorescents ticked, footsteps thumped from the library above. The air carried dust, sweat, and the tang of stale takeaway.

Simon wasn't there for coursework. He was there for the network — a living organism of servers and permissions, riddled with blind spots. A forgotten guest account here, an unsecured printer queue there. Every flaw was a thread to tug, and the system shifted when he pulled.

Outside, wind scraped along the lanes. A bicycle bell rang twice. Cambridge had its own rhythm: bells, boots, bikes, protests. Simon matched it — long nights, quiet days, his private map of vulnerabilities sharpening by the hour.

Julian was everywhere. At ease in the Union bar. Buried in library stacks. Remembering names as easily as weaknesses. He never entered a conversation without knowing how he meant to leave it.

At a Magdalene basement party, Simon met Sophie Patel. A battered boombox looped All Together Now by The Farm between bursts of the Happy Mondays. A Stone Roses poster curled from damp plaster. Cigarette smoke climbed toward a low ceiling. Sophie leaned against the wall, pint untouched, watching the dancers with a detachment that made people uneasy.

At a table sagging under cider and paper cups, she spoke first.

"You're Thorne's quiet friend."

"And you are?"

"Sophie Patel. Law. You like computers."

"Something like that."

She smiled, filing the answer away like evidence. Her law notes were full of clipped phrases — clause, em dash, verdict. That cadence would outlive Cambridge.

Later, when the music cut and the lights came up, they were still talking. When Simon mentioned how easily the college's servers gave way, she tilted her head.

"Maybe they aren't trying to keep you out."

The remark lingered — half-warning, half-invitation. Simon looked away, but it stayed with him, heavy as a lock already turning.

As he left, the corridor smelled of spilt cider and damp coats. A step behind him, deliberate.

"She's sharper than she looks. Pay attention."

Julian stepped forward, his smile faint, his eyes unreadable. For a moment, Simon wondered whether the warning was for Sophie's sake — or his.

Chapter 3

The Union bar pulsed with the Friday crush — taps hissing, plates clattering, voices colliding in waves. Smoke clung low to coats and hair. The air was sour with the scent of hops and tallow. Simon took the wall seat, pint glass sweating onto the wood.

Across the room, students argued about Maastricht, their voices snagging on ragged choruses. A girl in a red scarf declared that history only mattered when it spilled into headlines. Simon half-listened, storing fragments the way he mapped servers — arguments as entry points, silences as ports left open.

Julian leaned across the table, whisky in hand. He eased the window latch into place with deliberate care. The click cut through the noise; order collapsed into argument.

"In Brussels, during Maastricht, one man said, 'Bureaucrats will decide everything now.'" Julian's tone was smooth, measured. "He was wrong. They won't decide anything. They'll decide the story."

The words hit Simon harder than he admitted. He thought of his uncle's street in Belfast — the story written in bullets, not headlines.

Julian rotated the glass until the amber made a line along the napkin.

"Across town, a banker told my father, 'BCCI? The accounts didn't vanish. They moved.'"

The weight beneath his words wasn't history but something alive, tugging at Simon like an undertow under calm water. Julian let the noise swell, then dropped his line.

"There's someone who'd like to meet you. Dr Malcolm Royston. Connected. The kind of man who feels the current bend before the tide shifts."

The name sounded rehearsed, as if Julian had practised it to perfection. Later, Simon would wonder if this was the first tug of the leash.

Simon frowned. "And what does he want with me?"

"What he wants doesn't matter. What he offers does."

Julian's cufflink caught the light as he nudged his glass by a degree, satisfied only when symmetry returned.

"You like puzzles," he said. "Royston has a few you won't find in the lab."

Simon turned his pint, foam collapsing into rings. He should have brushed it off, laughed at the performance. But the name hung like static in the air — charged, inevitable.

At the bar, a man folded his newspaper and left his glass unfinished. No student's hurry. Collar raised. Eyes never quite lifting. Their gazes met for a fraction — impersonal, measuring — then he was gone.

Julian didn't watch the man leave. He watched Simon instead, calm as ever, smile precise. The game had already shifted.

———

Outside, lamps hummed over wet pavement. Smoke bled from the door as Simon stepped into the cold. The latch snapped behind him. A lock, clean and final.

Chapter 4

The Hills Road building didn't advertise itself. Mid-century brick. A few parking bays. An oak security door with a digital keypad decades newer than the façade. Behind drawn blinds, fluorescents glowed, illuminating dust drifting like forgotten words.

Simon sat in the café opposite, bitter espresso cutting through the murmur of students and commuters. Afternoon light pooled on scratched Formica, brittle as foil.

Julian appeared at his shoulder without warning.

"You're watching Hills Road."

"The archives Royston mentioned."

"You've started already."

"Of course."

At first, it was reconnaissance. Mapping the IP range through a cable spliced to ivy. Tracing dial-up handshakes in and out. The keypad code rotated daily — four digits. He couldn't see the numbers, but he saw the ancient controller spitting them, firmware unpatched since the '80s, left exposed because no one cared to secure it.

Every page he turned left a stain, as if the data itself carried secrets someone wanted forgotten. At Royston's name, Julian grew still, guarded, as if handling instructions he'd never chosen

The first night, silence.

The second, his script screeched parity errors so loud through his headphones that the girl behind the counter looked up before he killed the line.

The third, he fixed the timings, slipped the rate limit, and found a directory tree: user accounts, backup schedules, the faint pulse of a system forgotten because everyone thought it harmless.

Three nights in, he was inside. Not the building — the server. Tree. Logs. Headers. Nothing dramatic. Nothing illegal. But the line between looking and touching was seconds, not ethics.

One daemon lingered in the process list — not his, not admin. A watcher. It didn't probe, didn't block. It only logged. He realised then he wasn't invisible. He was being tolerated.

At the admin desk the next morning, the duty tech's eyes lingered too long when he slid Simon's warning slip across the counter. Not irritation, not pity — something withheld. As if the punishment wasn't his to enforce. As if someone higher had already decided Simon's future.

Later that week, Julian dropped into his narrow room. Sophie sat folded in the corner, Bonfire of the Vanities in her lap, gaze ticking between them like a metronome.

"Royston wants a walk-in," Julian said. "No copies. No traces. Eyes only."

"That's not simple—" Simon began.

"It's never simple," Julian cut him off. "That's why it matters."

Sophie closed her book, finger holding the page.

"You two sound like you're planning a burglary." Julian's smile was almost pleasant.

"Planning is dull. We're exploring possibilities."

Her eyes stayed on Simon.

"Possibilities have owners," she said softly. "And alarms."

Julian glanced around. A spoon on the desk sat off-centre. With one finger, he nudged it straight. With two, he adjusted Simon's collar.

"Some things demand symmetry."

The phrase landed heavily. Simon knew he'd hear it again.

When they left the stairwell, a door closed somewhere down the corridor. The hinge gave a faint groan, then silence.

Chapter 5

The streets lay quiet, broken only by a bus rattling past, windows fogged, passengers glowing under sodium haze. Headlamps swept across wet cobbles. For a moment, Simon thought they slowed — like eyes lingering before moving on.

Simon wore a plain black jacket and gloves that were thin enough for the keypad. Julian had insisted: no phones, no ID. Only a slim reporter's notebook in Simon's pocket, pages blank.

They met Royston at a bus shelter two streets away. Leaflets plastered the timetable — a Poll Tax protest, an Amnesty lecture on the Gulf crisis. His collar was up, his felt hat dripping. On one hand, he rolled a fountain pen, uncapped, with green ink.

"You have twenty minutes," he said. "After that, the guard makes his round."

Julian nodded as if they were planning a train journey.

"And what are we looking for?"

"You'll know it when you see it."

The keypad was a model Simon knew by schematic. Four seconds to trigger, three to tease the relay. The oak door unlocked, clicking loudly in the rain.

Inside: dry air, a faint chemical tang. Rows of metal shelving. Boxes labelled in the same stolid font used since the '70s. Somewhere above, a bulb hummed too loudly. Simon moved fast, cross-checking the wall index with the directory in his head. Julian stayed close, listening for a guard's tread.

The file was small. Buff folder. Red string. Inside: photos, typed reports, names. Ministry letterhead. Dates from the late '80s.

Simon froze. Images of soldiers blurred mid-burst — muzzle flashes suspended, smoke hanging above low buildings, bodies scattered across churned verges.

The scene bled into memory. Not paper. Belfast. His uncle's street. Wet brick. Mud-slick verge. Faces turning away. The silence after shots.

But the report in his hands — these pictures — weren't Northern Ireland.

Julian leaned close. "Is this Linton?"

Simon said nothing. His eyes fixed on the last page: a memo stamped CLASSIFIED – EYES ONLY. Linton, Cambridgeshire. An 'operational mishap.' Civilian deaths. Memo dated 12 March 1991.

Julian whispered, voice thin as wire. "We shouldn't have seen this."

Upstairs, an oak door closed — it was like a gunshot in the silence.

Then footsteps.

They were gone in ninety seconds — file replaced, keypad reset, rain falling fine as mist. Royston had vanished.

Julian didn't speak until they reached the edge of the college, music leaking from a nearby bar.

"Now you understand why some doors are locked." His voice was calm, rehearsed.

"It doesn't matter what we saw. What matters is whose version survives."

Rain needled Simon's face. Sophie's words surfaced: possibilities have owners.

Julian's expression gave nothing away. Only the exact symmetry of collar and cuffs, controls as armour against consequence.

On Hills Road, the oak door wore a new escutcheon and a keypad hood that hadn't been there on Friday. A contractor's van idled with no markings, condensation feathered the windscreen, though the air was mild. The porter across the street told a cyclist, "Just routine," but watched the door like it might answer back.

By Sunday, Cambridge felt altered. The air sharp with woodsmoke, bicycle chains still wet. But the photographs replayed in Simon's head — soldiers, blurred bodies, bureaucratic neatness masking disaster. His uncle's street had looked the same. The memory weighed heavier than the file.

The radiator ticked in bursts.

"Royston called," Julian said quietly, turning a fountain pen until the cap sat flush. "He's pleased."

"Pleased we broke into a government archive?"

"Pleased we proved we could."

Simon almost asked why Royston wanted the information in the file, but stopped. The question felt like an anchor ready to drag him under.

Sophie arrived mid-conversation, coat still on, scarf tight. She dropped her bag onto the desk, scattering papers.

"You've been absent."

"Busy."

"Doing what?"

"Nothing you'd care about."

She opened the FT, nail tracing a line. A subcommittee on defence oversight. Phrase: recent operational incidents in the East of England.

"'East of England' is a euphemism," she said. "They use it when they're hiding something near Cambridge. Which town?"

She asked questions like cross-examination — tight, clipped, leaving no room to dodge.

Julian's eyes flicked to Simon, quick as a blade.

"Coincidence," he said smoothly.

"Or not," Sophie replied. Her tone was measured, sharper than Simon had ever heard.

———

That night, alone, Simon unlocked his hacked copies of the Hills Road logs. Floppies stacked, indexed only in his notebook. Outgoing connections traced: modem handshakes to London. Registry name meaningless. Location: Whitehall.

If Sophie was right, then this puzzle already belonged to someone else. And Royston, and whoever he worked for, knew he'd touched it.

The glow of the screen cut his face. The lock had turned. And he was inside it.

Chapter 6

Sophie had warned him: every possibility belonged to someone. Watching Julian drift closer to Royston's orbit, Simon wondered if she had seen this coming.

By midweek, Julian was already slipping deeper into that circle. Simon glimpsed him between lectures — always with older men in sharp suits, the kind who never carried books. They leaned in too close when they spoke; Julian listened intently, never pulling away.

Sophie noticed too.

"He's networking," she said one evening from Simon's bed, legs folded beneath her, eyes on his screen as code crawled down.

"He's… busy," Simon replied without looking up.

Her gaze narrowed. "Not student busy. That's cultivated. You don't give away smiles like that unless they've already bought the time."

The words pressed, quiet but precise. Simon almost asked what she meant, but the cursor blinked — six months of outbound traffic from Hills Road. London at the hub. Lines to Brussels, Washington, and one odd link to a private number in rural Norfolk. The modem shrieked, then stilled; a single timestamp held. His throat tightened. Norfolk wasn't random. Norfolk meant reach.

Sophie leaned forward, elbows on knees. "That Norfolk number. You've seen it before."

He hesitated.

She tilted her head. "Patterns repeat, Simon. Don't tell me you haven't noticed."

The thought landed heavier than she knew. If every possibility belonged to someone, then this number was a flag planted — ownership marked in the middle of nowhere.

He snapped the notebook shut and stood. The room felt smaller. Nothing obvious had changed — the laundry, the books — yet the pencil jar sat slightly off-centre. A faint whiff of tobacco lingered where no one smoked. The window latch was in the second notch, not the first.

"Sophie," he said evenly, "did you touch my desk?"

"No." She frowned. "Should I have?"

He shook his head, as if it were nothing, but the air pressed closer. His hand brushed the folded photograph in his pocket — his cousin's grin fading when the soldiers came. A reminder that locks had failed once before.

Sophie stood and snapped the latch back into place with a click. "If someone's testing your boundaries, let them think you're unaware," she said. "I'll ask a friend in telecoms about that Norfolk line. Quietly. You're not the only one who can pull threads."

"Come on," she added, grabbing his coat. "Two minutes."

She cut down Trinity Lane without warning, paused in a shop window's warped glass, then doubled back along the railings. A man with a newspaper hesitated, then turned the wrong way.

"Not the cameras," Sophie murmured. "The gaps."

Back at the door, her smile was small, satisfied. "If you're chasing that line, don't even think about doing it alone."

Chapter 7

Norfolk wasn't random. The number had repeated too often, too neatly, to be chance.

Simon boarded the Saturday train alone, ignoring Sophie's warning. Her contact had traced the number east, to a lane where strangers never went unnoticed.

From the station, he cycled miles beneath a slate-grey sky. Hedgerows stripped bare. Fields sodden. The kind of place where visitors were clocked before they even arrived.

Number 14 waited at the end of the lane: a converted barn, slate roof, high gates.

A low hum bled into the air, faint but constant — like a refrigerator in an otherwise silent house.

Simon leaned his bike against a fence and walked the perimeter. A thin telephone wire sagged into the building.

Ordinary. Beside it ran a second cable, thicker, feeding a utility box on the verge. Too much capacity for a cottage. A relay.

The floodlight above buzzed, casing rattling with static. Orange glare shattered across the lane like broken glass.

He set his laptop on a low wall, clipped a coupler to the line, and began wardialling the village exchange. Numbers fell silent one by one, until every few minutes the line at No. 14 flickered alive: handshake, stitched data, then gone. Too short for chatter. Long enough for orders.

"Lose something?"

The voice came from behind.

A man in his sixties stood at the gate. Tweed jacket, cable-knit jumper, hands buried in his pockets. No smile. His gaze dropped to the laptop, then back to Simon.

"Just passing through," Simon said.

"Not many pass through here. Especially with kit like that."

The air tasted metallic, like iron filings. Simon forced himself to keep still.

He tried a shrug. "Line's crackly where I'm staying. Thought it might be clearer out here."

The man's expression didn't shift. "Clarity costs more than you think."

Simon closed the laptop slowly, willing his hand not to shake. The man didn't move aside, didn't threaten. He only watched long enough that Simon felt the weight of it on his back as he mounted his bike.

The gate latch clicked shut as he pedalled away.

That night, Julian called.

"Royston says you've been poking around. Decide whose side you're on."

Simon didn't answer.

Later, in his room, an envelope waited beneath the door. Inside was a photograph of him and Sophie, mid-laugh at the Union bar.

On the back, in her handwriting: Don't disappear completely.

A thumbprint smudged the corner — not his. The ink on the edge was damp.

Her smile in the photo caught him off guard. He could almost hear the laugh that had made him look up, sharp and bright against the Union's smoky air.

He slid the photo into his pocket and listened. The corridor breathed old-building sounds: pipes ticking, a cistern refilling, the porter's radio murmuring. Then a softer thing — a trace of cologne that wasn't his, and the chair set a fraction from the desk, a caster angled outward.

Simon reset the chair and sat on the bed, hands flat to the coverlet. The Norfolk number pulsed in his head, each flicker a call and response.

He told himself he had seen enough.

He told himself he would leave it alone.

He didn't believe either sentence.

CHAPTER 8

Simon sat back in the chair, pulse tight in his throat. Norfolk hadn't been erased. But it had been silenced, for now.

By Monday, he was certain someone had been in his room. The laundry lay where he'd left it, but the cable was wound too neatly, the stage reset. His chair had shifted — half an inch from the wall, a caster turned askew. A trace of cigarette smoke lingered — sharp, foreign, unmistakably expensive.

The longer he stared, the more he saw. A biro that had always rolled to the desk's edge now lay centred above his notebook. The wardrobe door rested a sliver open, though he remembered shutting it with a kick. All of it deliberate.

He said nothing to Sophie. She was already uneasy with the silence he'd carried back from Norfolk, her questions circling but never spoken. He let them hang.

The next day she mentioned a man lingering outside the law faculty, cigarette in hand, pretending to study the noticeboard long after everyone else had gone. He wasn't dressed like a student — too neat, too polished — and when she passed, he half-smiled, as if the posters truly amused him. She laughed it off in the telling, but Simon caught the edge in her voice — the same unease he'd felt himself.

In the computer lab, something had shifted. A machine he'd run scripts on now demanded new credentials. Two logins revoked — no note, no admin trail. Just subtraction. The strip-lights ticked to a higher pitch, the room's hum turning from background to verdict.

Julian's smile was precise, without warmth. He toyed with a silver cigarette case, angling the reflection until it threw a glint onto the ceiling beam. He repeated the motion until it landed in the same place twice, satisfied only when symmetry returned.

"You're drawing attention," he said. "Royston dislikes attention."

"Tell him to stop leaning on my door."

The smile thinned. "If someone had been to your room, Simon, you wouldn't be asking questions. You'd be missing answers." The words hung longer than the smile, heavier for their calm delivery.

That night, instinct pulled Simon back to the secure drive of the Hills Road logs. The Norfolk number was gone, scrubbed clean. In its place, a new number and location surfaced — an office not half a mile from college. He didn't need Sophie to remind him — the logs made it clear. He was trespassing on ground someone else already owned.

He leaned back, listening. Cambridge pressed in. The wind off Mill Road carried coal smoke, stale hops, and the faint electronic tang of a screen left on in an empty room.

On his machine, a new daemon squatted in his process list — [kstat] — quiet, not probing; just watching. Simon scrolled, heart thudding. It hadn't been there last week. Someone had left it like a fingerprint, a presence he could neither erase nor ignore.

Cambridge felt smaller now, its walls closing in, every door tested to see how easily it shut.

The law faculty emptied in drifts, papers tucked under arms, heels clicking toward the bar. Sophie stayed back, crouched by the noticeboard where thumbtacks pinched curling announcements.

Simon found her there, eyes flicking not at the paper but at the glass.

"There's a blind spot," she said softly. "The camera doesn't cover the doorway. I watched three people step through without being clocked."

He frowned. "You've been watching the watchers?"

She shrugged, a trace of a smile. "Isn't that your job?"

Before he could answer, a porter crossed the court with deliberate slowness, glancing once, then again. Sophie tilted her head, marking it without a word.

"See?" she murmured. "You're not the only one mapping patterns."

Then she straightened, slipping her bag onto her shoulder, leaving Simon to wonder whether she'd just helped him — or warned him.

Chapter 9

Julian was already at the corner table when Simon arrived, pint half-drained, napkin aligned with military precision, a private insistence on order.

He hadn't come to drink. He'd come to make Simon choose.

The pub air was dense with sour beer soaked into the floorboards, smoke clinging to curtains. Condensation streaked the windows, streetlamps outside warped into molten halos.

Julian's cufflinks caught the light as he looked up.

"Royston needs a decision," he said. "You're either in, or you're out."

Simon kept his eyes on the froth clinging to his glass. "In what?"

"The room. The list. The current that pulls everything you've been chasing. You stop running solo. You work through me. In return, you'll see names and networks you thought were shadows. Ministers. Officers. Contractors. Threads tied off before you ever saw the knot."

"And if I'm out?"

Julian's smile was small, without kindness.

"Then you walk away knowing less than you do now. It isn't a club, Simon. It feeds. On people like us. Always has. Royston doesn't offer twice. And he doesn't forgive hesitation."

Simon thought of Norfolk. The shuttered building. The signal that shouldn't have reached his line. The man Sophie said had lingered too long at the law faculty noticeboard. Not just him anymore.

He could walk. He could stop.

But the current had already taken him.

"If I'm in," he murmured, "I keep my own keys."

Julian didn't blink. For a heartbeat too long, his eyes held Simon's — not just weighing him, but something closer, almost tender, quickly shuttered.

"Some doors will stay locked. For your own good."

A glass rattled on the bar. Coins clattered into the till. Simon realised he'd been holding his breath, then let it out.

He didn't sleep. The cursor blinked on the empty terminal until dawn, a silent metronome of unease.

They met again in the quad, the flagstones slick from night rain. The morning smelled of wet ivy and diesel from a passing truck.

"I'm in," Simon said.

Julian's smile was quiet, assured. Then, a pause — just long enough to weigh him.

"Good. Royston will be pleased."

"But with conditions," Simon added, his voice steady. "I work using my own kit. I keep parallel access to anything I touch. You get results faster, cleaner, without alarms. That's the deal."

Julian tilted his head, as if calibrating the words.

"We monitor our own."

"I'm counting on it."

That afternoon, the first task arrived: a probe on a London consultancy. On paper, routine. Between the lines, one board member was a retired brigadier with defence ties.

Simon worked from his room, blinds drawn, air thick with solder fumes and instant coffee. He mapped the network, flagged vulnerabilities, and slipped through a forgotten port in the gateway filter. Before logging out, he left himself a hidden login — a second .rhosts entry buried in an archive no admin would ever open.

One key for them. One key for him.

That night, Julian called.

"Royston says you're efficient."

"Tell him I like puzzles."

From the corridor outside, a bolt rattled faintly, though no one passed his door. The sound carried him back to childhood — nights when locks meant nothing, and someone else held the key.

The game was his now. Or so he needed to believe.

Chapter 10

The consultancy job should have ended cleanly. Royston had the vulnerability report. Julian delivered the praise. Simon could have walked away.

But the hidden login was still live.

On a quiet Thursday evening, while Cambridge drifted toward pubs and libraries, Simon logged back in.

At first, routine traffic — project updates, budget queries, administrative memos. Then, buried in a cipher-locked archive, a folder marked simply: Client X.

Inside: procurement contracts stamped CONFIDENTIAL — MOD. Terse correspondence routed through the same relay chain he'd traced before. Different property. Same pattern.

One invoice listed only "special consignments" — no item codes, just initials, approvals buried among freight tonnage and customs forms. Another memo authorised escort costs under welfare budgets. Language reduced to numbers and routes. A destination repeated: Linton, Cambridgeshire. A signature scrawled beneath: M. Royston.

The hairs on his arms lifted. He copied everything to his secure drive and logged out.

The screen flickered — almost too quick to catch. A knock on the back door he'd buried deep, the one no admin should ever find. Not random. Deliberate. A junior admin account blinked in his trace — scapegoated by the intrusion, its password changed two minutes before the knock.

They'd salted the path. He'd stepped anyway.

His hands shook once — the only time he let them — before he stilled them on the desk.

Ten hours later, the small cost arrived, neat as a receipt: his lab credentials were suspended for "usage anomaly," and the duty tech pretended not to know why. In the consultancy's logs, a silent new rule appeared — an audit daemon (watchd) watching for his signature. Someone was already writing the story of his trespass.

He almost stopped. Sophie's voice rose in memory: Maybe they weren't trying to keep you out.

The thought pinned him. He pressed on.

That night, Julian arrived without warning. No knock. Just the door easing shut.

"If Royston thinks you're holding out, he won't just cut you off. He'll unmake you, Simon. Piece by piece."

In the morning, an envelope slid under his door — a memo on Whitehall letterhead, dated two weeks earlier, referring to a "routine defence review" at Linton. The file hash he'd kept proved otherwise: it had been created yesterday. A provable lie. A test. He burned the copy and kept the hash — a private counter. If Royston intended to invent reality, Simon would keep the receipts.

The radiator ticked in uneven bursts. The thrill of discovery still burned — and now it bit back.

The relay wasn't finished. Someone knew.

Chapter 11

The call was brief.

"Tomorrow. Ten sharp. Wear something that doesn't look like you've been living in a cupboard," Julian said, and hung up.

The address led to a Georgian townhouse off Parker's Piece — black railings, brass numerals polished to a shine. A woman in a soot-dark suit opened at the first ring and took him up a narrow stair that smelled of beeswax and old paper. The air was curated, the kind that asked for quieter footsteps.

The study was a box of order. Books along three walls. A clock that didn't announce itself. Royston sat behind a desk the size of a billiard table, spectacles low, a Swan fountain pen uncapped beside a ledger where a line of green ink had just settled.

"Arkwright," he said, tasting the syllables. "You've caused disruption."

"I get curious," Simon replied.

"Curiosity is a resource. Properly managed, it yields. Unmanaged, it leaks." Royston didn't raise his voice; he didn't need to. "Norfolk, for instance."

Something clicked tight behind Simon's ribs. Royston left the word — "Norfolk" — like a pin on a map. Simon didn't move to take it out. Silence lengthened. Not a gap — a test.

He set the pen down with surgical care. "The police won't trouble you, Mr Arkwright. Curiosity like yours isn't punished. It's repurposed. I prefer to cultivate it before others do."

"I'm not interested in surveillance for its own sake," Royston went on, tone stripped of pretence. "You work for me now, whether you admit it or not. You'll have puzzles. Some wrapped in paper, some in barbed wire. You'll take both."

Simon nodded once. He was already mapping where his own access could remain hidden.

Royston noticed, but pretended not to. A corner of his mouth shifted — not approval, not quite.

"Good. Tell me what you've found that you haven't told Thorne."

Simon met his eyes.

"I'll need context. Scope. Purpose."

Royston capped the pen with a soft click. The gesture was neat, final.

"At least you understand the cost of speaking," he said. "Keep that instinct. It may keep you useful."

He slid a single envelope across the desk. Heavy paper. No markings. A mission brief tucked inside.

"Start with this. Deliver clarity, not noise. If you fabricate, I'll know. If you hoard, I'll also know."

Simon didn't reach for it yet. When he did, the envelope was lighter than expected, yet his hand closed on it as if it carried weight.

"And Thorne?" he asked.

"Thorne is a channel," Royston said.

He watched Simon the way a collector studies an acquisition — deciding if it belonged.

"You're clever," he said. "Clever men survive only if they learn where to stop."

On the credenza, a matte case opened and snapped shut. No serials. No labels. Royston never looked. He didn't need to. Simon couldn't help himself — the prototypes were irresistible.

Royston set the pen aside. The ink line was dry now.

"Go. Take the case — you may find the contents useful."

The woman in the soot-dark suit was waiting at the landing. On the stair, the house exhaled its wax and leather again, the hush of old bindings. Outside, air moved colder, a thin smell of diesel drifting off the grass on Parker's Piece.

Behind him, a door strained — not a groan, more the creak of a hinge tested and a latch settling in place. He didn't turn. He already knew which way it closed.

CHAPTER 12

The email arrived the next morning. No greeting. No signature.

Just,

Subject: Kendrick & Vale – Internal Review

(uuencoded client list below; decode with uudecode)

Simon knew the name — a discreet advisory firm in Cambridge, tucked into a terrace he'd passed a hundred times.

The brief was sparse: assess security posture. Deliver findings to Royston. No other distribution.

He stripped the blocks back into cleartext in seconds, command-line fluency turning the jagged characters into names and numbers.

By midday, he'd already mapped their network. An NFS export left world-readable DAT backups stacked and unlabelled. Passwords so thin they felt like invitations.

Outside the window, sunlit buses rattled past, their flip-dot destination boards flaring through the glass. For a moment, the lab felt dry, bright, too sharp — the kind of light that made secrets seem impossible. But the ledger glowed on his screen, refusing to dissolve in sunshine.

In a segregated folder marked Legacy Clients, he found transaction histories stretching back fifteen years. Transfers through trusts, holding companies, and foundations that posed as philanthropic. Buried among them were names he recognised: mid-level politicians, donors, advisers.

One in particular stopped him cold — a backbench MP who had resigned years earlier over an undeclared stake in a defence contractor. Simon remembered the headline on the breakfast table, his uncle shaking his head, muttering that nothing ever changed. And here was the man again, hidden in the ledgers like a bad penny. One transfer for £38,400 on 12 February 1991 sat like a thumbprint in the margin.

£38,400. Not enough to topple a government.

Just enough to own one man.

Not a lapse—an instrument. The books were the leverage.

He sealed the folder into his private archive, layering ciphers until even he might struggle to reopen them. Royston would never see it.

The thought came unbidden: whose hands did this money really serve? He tightened the lock anyway, as though secrecy were his only armour. Some doors he would keep for himself.

Outside Kendrick & Vale, a white panel van idled too quietly for its size, condensation feathering the windscreen, though the air was mild.

By evening, Julian was at his door. The corridor smelled faintly of polish, as if someone had already been inside.

"Royston says you work quickly," Julian said. "He's pleased."

Simon leaned on the frame, concealing the notebook in his pocket. "Good. Let's keep it that way."

Julian's eyes lingered — sharp, weighing him — before sliding off with deliberate ease.

The smile was faint, but it carried the weight of a warning.

Chapter 13

Three days later, Simon reopened the Legacy Clients. Long enough for Royston's attention to drift. Not long enough for the data to stale.

It was October 1991. Rain streaked the dormer window, the city muffled under damp air. Simon traced transactions with the care of a watchmaker, fingers steady despite the quickening in his chest.

Inheritance transfers. Land purchases. Offshore trusts. At first, noise. Then the pattern emerged.

Multiple accounts converged on a Gibraltar holding company. From there, money bled into a London consultancy — the same name that had surfaced in Norfolk. Out again in precise disbursements: charities, think tanks, niche media outfits.

The timing was surgical. Each burst of transfers preceded a political shift: a committee chair resigning, a bill stalling, a minister suddenly off-script. On 3 May 1991, £250,000 pulsed through Gibraltar to the consultancy. Three days later, a committee vote flipped without explanation. In July, another flow — £400,000 this time — and a junior minister's speech on defence procurement was withdrawn at the last minute. The record showed he had been in perfect health.

Simon built a map — dates, flows, outcomes — until the shape became undeniable.

The ledger blurred. He thought of his uncle at the kitchen table in Belfast, voice low, smoke curling from a damp cigarette. Politicians don't care who dies. They care who signs the cheques.

Sophie noticed the folded photo in his notebook.

"Who's that?"

He closed it too fast.

"My cousin."

"Still close?"

A pause.

"No. He carried something that was mine. Cost him more than it cost me."

Her eyes softened, then sharpened. "So don't let it happen twice."

This wasn't leverage anymore. It was circuitry. Money as a command signal, pulsing through the system, invisible yet decisive.

Recipients included a policy institute ghostwriting ministerial papers, and a cultural foundation with discreet defence ties. None of them random. Every node had purpose.

He sealed the ledger behind fresh layers of PGP encryption and pulled it offline. A floppy labelled only with a blank date slipped into a case taped beneath the desk.

In a dead-drop folder, he typed: If anything happens to me, send this to every name pulled from the Legacy Clients.

The choice pressed like a lock beneath his hands. Burn it, and nothing changed. Release it, and maybe everything did.

He saw his uncle's street again — brick slick with rain, silence imposed. He saw his cousin's face, folded in his pocket for too many years, punished because Simon had stayed silent once.

He tore the photo free. For a moment, he almost put it back. Then he let it fall, a pale blur against the dark floor. Not this time.

The cursor blinked. A threat. A promise. Both.

For a moment, Sophie's handwriting surfaced in his mind — Don't disappear completely. The words pressed against him like a weight. He remembered the curve of her smile when she teased him, the edge in her voice when she warned him. He pushed it down, saved the folder, and shut the drive.

The room was silent except for the radiator ticking. His reflection in the dark window looked older than the week had any right to make him.

At midnight, his pager buzzed once. The vibration rattled the desk, sharp in the quiet. He unfolded the slip, thumb brushing static from the display.

A number. Then a code.

We need to talk. Alone. – J

Simon sat back, the pager warm in his hand. Outside, Cambridge shifted in its sleep — bicycles clattering late on Mill Road, a porter's radio cutting out mid-song, footsteps on wet flagstones fading into silence.

Somewhere, a lock turned, and a door closed.

Chapter 14

They met at dusk on the footpath by Jesus Green.

The river ran pitch-dark, the air sharp with wet leaves. Cyclists hissed past, their lights stuttering in the gloom. Somewhere upstream, a dog barked, the sound carrying thinly across the water.

Julian leaned against the rail. No suit tonight, just a wool coat, collar up, hands buried deep in his pockets.

"You're getting reckless," he said without looking at Simon.

"Careful is boring."

Julian's eyes flicked toward him. "Kendrick & Vale isn't just a consultancy. Norfolk wasn't a blip. You're touching the same circuitry from two angles, and Royston hates crossed wires."

Simon leaned beside him, breath visible in the cold. "You know what that circuitry actually is?"

Julian hesitated, then nodded. "Influence. Not money — power. You saw the names. The timing."

"I mapped them."

Julian's mouth twitched, almost a smile. "Of course you did."

Halogen lamps bled colour from the water. Downriver, a lone rower's oar slapped the surface, steady as a metronome. The rhythm carried, insistent, like a pulse beneath the city.

Julian's voice dropped. "There's a limit to how far I can shield you. Push past it and you'll burn. I've seen it."

"Why warn me?"

His smile turned inward, almost mocking. "Maybe I like the way you think. Maybe I don't want to watch another bright mind crushed into compliance."

The streetlights buzzed to life one by one, their glow softening the edges of the path. Simon's voice was low but certain. "I'll finish the map, with or without you."

Julian didn't answer. But he didn't walk away, either. He watched the river for a long moment, dark water bending light into fractured patterns.

"When I was ten, we lived in Brussels," he said at last. "My father sat in a room where men decided which countries would be heard, and which would be ignored. I sat outside with the other children. When the doors closed, we stopped existing. That was the lesson; silence isn't neutral. It's imposed."

Simon stayed quiet, letting the words settle. The memory had sharpened Julian's voice, but what lay beneath was older, more dangerous than nostalgia. He pictured the boy left in the corridor, listening for decisions through oak doors, learning early that exclusion was a weapon.

"He never forgave the closed door," Simon said carefully.

Julian's gaze hardened. "No. I learned to close them first."

For once, his symmetry faltered. A cufflink had slipped a degree off true. He saw it but didn't fix it. The imperfection lingered between them, a fracture he allowed.

His tone softened, then turned steely again. "I decided then I'd never sit on the wrong side. Control isn't optional. It's survival."

A gust stirred the leaves across the path, scattering them like a deck of cards. A cyclist swerved to avoid them, bell chiming once before fading into the dark.

Simon looked at Julian and realised the warning wasn't protection. It was recruitment.

Chapter 15

They worked on Royston's assignments like a chess problem.

Every official task was played straight — reports submitted, vulnerabilities flagged, no trace of extra moves. That was the board everyone could see. The other board — the one that mattered — never had a name.

Around them, the café murmured with the hiss of the espresso machine, cutlery scraping, voices dipping and rising. Every lull sharpened the air until they could hear their own pages turn.

Simon did the digging; Julian supplied the context. Random names in Simon's eyes snapped into shape when Julian connected them — a minister's aide, a media fixer, a corporate lobbyist with a direct line into Whitehall — all feeding the same beige desktop tower.

The map resolved: Gibraltar HoldCo → London consultancy → think tanks and media outlets → committee rooms. The pulses landed three days before outcomes — chairs resigned, votes flipped, ministers drifted off-script. Money wasn't influence; it was a command signal, invisible in daylight, decisive in motion.

It was delicate work. Probe too deep, and Royston's people saw the ripples. Probe too lightly, and the threads dissolved into noise.

After three weeks, Simon caught an anomaly: a payment sequence routed through Rotterdam. A logistics front, money shunted sideways, out of rhythm with Royston's loops.

Julian frowned at the printout, thumb nudging the edge into alignment before he spoke.

"That's not one of his."

"Then whose is it?"

Julian hesitated. "Someone he doesn't control. Which makes them dangerous."

The printout lay between them like a fault line. The café noise swelled and receded, a tide they no longer heard.

Back in Simon's room, a loan-only form sat under a mug ring: items listed by euphemism, return conditions in green ink. His gaze lingered on the scrawl. The old warning pressed in on him, heavy as drizzle — every possibility belongs to someone.

That night, he cipher-locked the Rotterdam lead, stashing it apart from the rest. If there was a piece on the board Royston didn't own, it might be the only one worth keeping.

He paused before closing the directory, checking the checksum twice. The file name was nothing but numbers, yet it carried the weight of a confession.

Two days later, his pager buzzed. The vibration startled him awake, rattling the desk lamp.

The slip glowed with clipped precision:

Lunch. The Eagle. Tomorrow. 1 PM.

Alone.

Simon stared at the message until the digits blurred. The Eagle was loud, crowded, and impossible to sweep. Not a trap, perhaps, but a stage. Whoever had chosen it wanted him seen.

CHAPTER 16

The Eagle was already half full when Simon arrived. Tourists jostled at the bar, their voices carrying above the hiss of taps and clatter of plates. Students crowded the tables, sleeves rolled, shouting half-arguments about exams and Maastricht. The air was heavy with cigarette smoke, fried food, and the yeast-sweet scent of beer sunk deep into the floorboards.

Royston had chosen the back booth. Not by accident.

A Swan pen lay on the folded newspaper, a dot of green drying where the tip had kissed the margin.

From there, he held sightlines on both doors, his coat folded with exactness beside him. No pint, no plate — only a glass of water sweating condensation against a neatly folded newspaper. Even in this chaos, he radiated stillness.

"Mr Arkwright." His tone was measured, almost pleasant. "Enjoying Cambridge?"

Simon slid into the opposite seat, ordering coffee when the waitress passed — something to anchor his hands. "Busy, mostly."

"Yes. You've been very busy." Royston's eyes never lowered to the paper he pretended to read. "Discretion, Mr Arkwright, isn't a word; it's a discipline. Some of my people forget that."

Simon forced himself to meet his gaze, steady. "If there's something you want to say, say it."

Royston's smile twitched but never reached his eyes. "Rotterdam."

Not noise. A stray pulse.

The word landed like a dropped weight between them.

The waitress set down Simon's cup, the saucer rattling faintly. Neither man acknowledged her.

Royston leaned forward, lowering his voice. "Most patterns in my world are intentional. A few are noise.

Rotterdam is neither. Which means you found something unscheduled. Initiative is admirable, in moderation."

Simon wrapped his hand around the coffee, more for cover than warmth. The steam curled into his face, metallic and bitter. "It was an anomaly. I noted it. That's all."

"Curiosity," Royston said softly, "becomes dangerous when it outruns discipline. And leaks, Mr Arkwright, invite consequences." He smoothed a crease from the newspaper with a single finger, eyes still locked on Simon. "Some doors don't open until you're invited. Knock too loudly, and the wrong person answers."

For a moment, the noise of the pub seemed to recede. Simon felt the beat of his pulse in his throat, the smell of fried food suddenly cloying, too close.

Royston stood, the booth releasing him like a shadow peeling from the wall. He adjusted his cuffs, straightened his coat, and the crowd seemed to part for him without effort — as if the room itself knew better than to obstruct his path.

"Enjoy your coffee," he said. "I'll be in touch."

When he rose, the glass left a ring. Beside it, the faintest smear of green.

Simon watched him go, the glass of water still sweating rings on the table. He lifted the coffee at last, swallowing hard. The bitterness clung to his tongue, refusing to leave.

Rotterdam no longer felt like a discovery. It felt like proof — proof that Royston was watching every move, and proof that Simon had just stepped into a game with pieces he couldn't yet see.

In the mirror behind the bar, a man pretended to study the taps and didn't blink.

Chapter 17

Simon took the overnight ferry from Harwich, folding himself into the ranks of hauliers and oil workers.

Rotterdam met him beneath a steel sky, the air thick with salt, diesel, and rain. Overhead, cranes loomed like watchtowers guarding mountains of containers.

From the derelict shell of a warehouse, binoculars to his face, Simon saw the difference. One pier stood apart. Men in plain jackets—no uniforms—posture too precise, gaze too steady. Every container vanished into a low warehouse; doors clanged shut before anyone outside could glimpse inside.

It all blurred into the familiar—borders, contraband, cargo—but sharper. Weighted.

Sophie's warning surfaced: every possibility has owners.

This wasn't code anymore. It was a design written before he arrived.

He almost pulled back.

A white cab eased from the yard, its trailer unmarked, plate flashing in orange vapour light. Headlights carved the rain-slick tarmac.

Simon followed the glow until it bled into darkness.

"You never know when to leave a thing alone."

Julian. Windbreaker zipped to the throat, soot-dark jeans, immaculate—as if he'd stepped out of a catalogue instead of a ferry terminal.

"You followed me," Simon said.

Julian's smile was faint. "You didn't think Royston would let you board a ferry without a shadow, did you?"

Simon said nothing.

"They don't have a name," Julian went on, eyes on the pier. "But just be aware, they've ended more people than you'll ever count."

He adjusted his bag strap. "At King's—remember the bursar's resignation? Everyone swore he admitted fraud."

"It was in the minutes," Simon said.

"No. It was in my minutes. One line, shifted by a week. Within days, he stopped denying it. Even he believed it in the end."

He nodded toward the pier. "That's the lesson. Truth matters less than the story people choose to believe. And these men—" a tilt of the chin "—have built an empire on the back of that."

The lorry was easy to shadow on the motorway. A rented hatchback, staying three cars back. Simon's palms sweated on the wheel, eyes flicking to the mirrors. The lorry never swerved, never slowed—ninety steady, middle lane.

"We shouldn't be doing this," Julian said.

"You shouldn't," Simon said. "I have to."

Two hours east, the lorry slipped off an unmarked exit and into a pine forest. Asphalt ended at a chained gate and a squat guardhouse.

After a brief exchange, the gate clanged open. The cab rolled through. The lock slammed shut.

Simon parked along the track, and they crept through the tree line. Resin stung the air, damp needles soft underfoot.

Through gaps in the branches: two warehouses, corrugated flanks under floodlight. Forklifts worked in a steady rhythm, shifting sealed crates from one building to the other. Along the wall, a bank of reefer units throbbed, ammonia sharp on the air—fans running hard, the kind of constant white noise that masks everything else.

The insulated bays behind them would hold a steady temperature and airflow even with the chillers idled down: circulation, not cold storage.

Beneath the mechanical racket lay something else, a deeper hum, pulsing steadily—it could be felt more than heard.

Julian's whisper was tight. "This is surveillance-grade suicide."

"Then it's a good thing I'm not staying."

Simon raised his camera, steadied, caught the plate, the yard lights, the sealed bay—enough to prove something existed.

They turned back through the pines.

The night hummed with machinery.

At the edge of the forest adjacent to the road, a payphone rang—once, twice.

Out of curiosity, Simon lifted the receiver. Static, then a measured voice: "Step away from Rotterdam. Last warning."

A faint relay click followed. The taped notice above the handset read: TARIEF PER 12 SEK.

The line cut.

Julian watched him return the handset.

For the first time, his features slipped out of symmetry.

He said nothing.

The silence between them outweighed the threat.

Chapter 18

The little Dutch hatchback carried them back toward Rotterdam in silence, headlights tunnelling through the wet dark. Lamps threw blurred halos across the tarmac.

"Whoever made that call wasn't Royston," Julian said at last. His tone carried no doubt. "And they won't warn twice."

"I can't stop now," Simon said.

Julian turned, profile sharp against the passing glow. "Do you hear yourself? This isn't a puzzle. It's a world where people disappear."

They pulled into a service station outside Dordrecht, sodium lamps buzzing in the drizzle. A handful of lorries idled under the yellow light. One saloon hadn't moved, its windscreen slick with rain, condensation fogging the inside.

While Julian went for coffee, Simon slid the grey Compaq LTE onto his lap. From his satchel, he drew the acoustic coupler, clipped it to the payphone receiver, and dialled a university access number he'd cached months earlier—an academic node in Tallinn that noticed nothing and remembered less, as secure and isolated as the world allowed.

The modem hissed and chattered. On the monochrome screen: queued UUCP batches bound for floppy, salted and split with parity, headers disguised as printer jobs, mirrored across half a dozen inboxes. Manifests were fractured and scattered, so no single copy could be smothered.

It wasn't instant. It didn't need to be. By morning, the packets would have replicated across nodes, checksums intact and timestamps set — stubborn proof in systems that liked to forget. And if something took him before he could act, there was a buried fallback: a second route, echoing a cadence Sophie would recognise. She'd follow the rhythm and find everything.

Julian returned with two paper cups. One glance at the screen was enough.

"You're setting a fuse," he said.

"I'm buying insurance," Simon replied.

They stood together at the edge of the car park, rain ticking against plastic lids. Julian's hand tightened around his cup.

"In Brussels," he said quietly, "A man was vanished for less. No body, no inquiry. My father called it diplomacy."

His voice thinned. "If they come for you, they come for me. I've lived with scars before, Simon — but the thought of losing you cuts deeper than any of them.

The saloon still hadn't moved. Its wipers remained frozen in the same half-arc.

Julian forced his face back into symmetry. The faint softening in his eyes was gone as quickly as it had appeared.

"If that fuse ignites," he said, "don't stop where we planned—run, and don't look back."

For a moment, his eyes softened again, despite himself. "And when it blows back—do you cut loose? Or drag me with you?"

Simon stared at the rain-smeared glow of the car park. He didn't answer.

CHAPTER 19

Julian had made a call after the Rotterdam warning—a back-channel number he kept for port fixers and men who still owed his father's name.

He gave Simon only the time: 11:00.

The contact arrived at 11:07.

The café's TV flickered with news from Yugoslavia. Vukovar smouldered, black smoke curling over white walls. At the bar, a traveller muttered he'd "just come back from hell." Names hung in the air: Sarajevo was tinder, one breath from flame.

The air reeked of wet wool and scorched grounds. Simon pressed his palm to the table grain, grounding himself as drizzle streaked the windows.

The man appeared as described—mid-forties, close beard, coat still wet. He ordered tea, no sugar, and slid into the booth.

"You have questions," he said in accented English.

"I have photographs," Simon replied. "And a lorry plate."

The man's mouth curved, not quite a smile. "Then you already hold more than most."

A package crossed the table. Inside: three blurred images—crates on a pallet, Cyrillic stamps, a customs seal from Novorossiysk.

Simon's eyes snagged on a cover sheet. A clipped phrase, out of place. Sophie's cadence—the way she annotated notes, the way she framed an argument. Impossible, yet there it was: printed in NATO grey, threaded through an official manifest.

His chest tightened, a flare of vertigo. She wasn't silent. She was still here. Active.

But how? Was she threading breadcrumbs toward him, trusting he'd catch the rhythm in her words? Or had someone higher lifted her patterns and bent them into a leash? If Sophie's hand was inside those files, then she was either reaching for him—or already owned.

"They don't ship every week," the contact said. "But always from the same origin, and always to that pier."

He hesitated, weighing Simon. "You're not the first to ask. An Englishman came months ago—clipped vowels, notes in green ink. He wanted manifests. Asked the same questions."

Royston.

"What's inside the containers?" Simon asked.

The man's gaze hardened. "You don't want to know."

Julian slid into the booth, whisky smoke clinging to his coat.

"He does," Julian said evenly. "And so do I."

The contact leaned closer, voice dropping beneath the rain. "Insulated bays. Biological. Not meat. Not plants."

He paused. "Alive."

The word hung there, heavier than smoke. Porcelain clicked against the saucer. The room seemed to hollow.

Simon felt the floor tilt with the silent promise of things that should never move. Across from him, Julian's fist closed under the table, tendons taut.

The contact drained his tea, buttoned his coat, and left. No farewell. No backward glance. Only absence, heavier than presence.

Chapter 20

As Simon rose to leave, a hand caught his sleeve.

Not the contact. Another man. Older, hair thinned and greying at the edges, coat heavy with the stale smoke of old cigarettes. He flashed a press card, its corners softened from years in a pocket.

"Before I tell you this," the man murmured, "the last person I passed a lead like this to… the papers called it suicide. At the funeral, the undertaker didn't bother to powder the ligature marks."

"So why give it to me?" Simon asked.

"Because you're closer than you realise. Better you than someone still naive enough to think none of this exists."

He drained what was left of his coffee. "Antwerp isn't the end. The crates don't stay. They're shifted again at Liège, on pharma trucks. White vans, clinical branding. Follow Antwerp to see the surface. Follow Liège to see who signs their names to it."

He hesitated, then added: "Your friend leaves fingerprints when she writes. Clause, em dash, clipped verb. Fingerprints on every line.

Maybe a warning. Maybe bait. Either way, she isn't invisible. Others will notice."

The words stuck like glass splinters. She wasn't silent. She was digging too—on the same threads, from another angle. Maybe signalling him. Maybe walking into the very hands he was chasing.

The thought pressed harder than the rain.

———

They left the café separately. Simon headed for the tram; Julian for the flat.

The plan: meet at Centraal by nine.

Rain slicked the cobbles as Simon crossed to the tram stop. From a doorway, tinny speakers leaked "All Together Now," warped and thin, as if Cambridge itself had seeped across the border.

A tram slid into the shelter, doors shuddering. In the glass he caught the outline twice—tall, black jacket, no umbrella. He stepped off before the tram moved. A side street swallowed him. The first man stayed. A second detached—shorter, heavier, keeping pace. When Simon cut through an alley, the second slowed, as if he'd expected it.

The hatchback was left in long-stay two blocks from the station. Simon tore the rental sticker from the windscreen and pocketed the paperwork. By the time they walked into the concourse, the car was just another shadow drowned in rain.

Julian was already at the station, windbreaker damp.

"We've got company," Simon said.

"Two on me," Julian replied. "Lost them near Damrak. They're not far behind."

They bought tickets for Brussels, then boarded a local to Haarlem instead. At Haarlem, they switched again, circling back toward Centraal to rinse their tail. The faces had changed. The attention hadn't.

They took a southbound train to Antwerp. The carriage smelled of damp coats and old coffee. The tannoy crackled overhead, names warped into static, half-swallowed before Simon could catch them. Each stop came with the long shriek of metal on metal, sharp enough to raise the hair on his arms. The windows shuddered with every curve, frames rattling like a code tapped out too fast. The floor thrummed with passing freight—a rhythm too close to the machinery hum in the forest. Ordinary sounds, he told himself. Ordinary. But his pulse was already matching their beat.

Across from him, Julian sat still, too still. His hand lay flat on his knee, fingers pressed hard to keep from twitching with each lurch of the carriage. Only the tension in his knuckles betrayed him. He tracked the corridor reflections in the glass without turning his head. Where Simon heard warning in every vibration, Julian measured silence, building symmetry out of the noise. A mask, practised and scarred, but a mask all the same.

Only once they crossed into Belgium did Julian speak.

"We can't go back to Cambridge. Not yet."

Mill Road ghosted through Simon's mind—buses, bikes, the kebab shop's late glow. He looked out at dark fields, reflections of stacked containers flickering in the window.

"Then we don't," he said. "We follow the cargo."

"Even if it buries us?"

Simon kept his gaze on the glass. "We're already under."

Chapter 21

Antwerp Centraal blurred with rain and sodium light. The lorry waited in the queue outside, plate unchanged, trailer blank. Simon fixed the number and tracked it toward the ring road, hopping a tram to keep pace. Julian broke off toward the freight yard—the surface layer their contact had named.

By the time floodlights burned overhead, both were at the fence.

The yard sprawled on Antwerp's edge—rails crisscrossing under floodlights that pressed everything into burnt orange and shadow. From a disused service road, they crouched behind the wire fence. Sodium lamps carved narrow corridors through the mist. Simon raised his binoculars, glass fogging in the cold.

"Same plate?" Julian asked, eyes still on the patrol paths.

"Same cab. Different trailer," Simon said, binoculars trembling in the cold.

Julian didn't look up. He nodded once, trusting the read.

The lorry idled at a siding while a crane lifted containers onto a flatbed. Most bore standard markings: one didn't.

"That's them."

Chains clattered. Two more followed—identical, unmarked, anonymous. Through the crane-cabin window, Simon caught a flicker of paper: a manifest stamped with a destination. He tightened the focus.

"Verona," he murmured.

Julian's gaze stayed on the guards and the arcs of light. "That's a long way from the North Sea."

"Which means there's a reason." Simon lowered the binoculars, the lenses damp with breath.

A floodlight swept the fence. They dropped flat. Footsteps crunched close. A flashlight paused where they'd been seconds before. Keys jingled. Then the beam moved on.

"Italy, then?" Julian whispered.

"Italy."

They slipped away before dawn, shadowing the flatbeds south through Luxembourg into Switzerland. By the time the lorries were shunted toward Basel, they were waiting at the station.

Basel station stank of coffee and wet concrete. They bought second-class tickets in cash, faces tilted from the lens above the desk. The carriage filled with murmurs in German, French, and Italian.

At the Swiss border, a guard's glance lingered too long. His thumb brushed the laminate of Simon's passport, eyes narrowing as if weighing the weight of paper against the silence between them. Then the stamp hit like a gavel.

Zurich blurred past in sodium glow. Travel ache settled in—the kind that seeped into bone. The Alps closed around them, tunnels swallowing the train before spitting it into valleys lit by scattered villages.

By dawn, they were on the Milan train, two carriages behind the flatbeds. When the line curved, Simon glimpsed the containers—three of them, chained tighter than anything else on the train, codes stenciled stark. Less like freight than prisoners.

"We get to Milan, then what?" Julian asked.

"Find the yard. See who takes delivery."

"And then?"

Simon didn't answer.

The train dove into another tunnel. Somewhere inside, the pitch under the wheels shifted—the faint groan of weight settling. Not ballast. Not steel. Too heavy. Too deliberate.

The sound vibrated up through his feet, into his ribs.

Julian glanced at him. "What?"

"Listen."

The sound wasn't the wheels on track. It was heavier, steadier—weight shifting inside steel. A resonance that didn't belong to freight.

It carried the memory of the pines: floodlit bays, reefer fans running hard to hide another noise. The same pulse, now moving east.

The train broke clear of the mountains. Valleys widened, rails straightened.

Milan drew closer.

By the time the flatbeds were diverted toward the freight terminal, Simon and Julian had already slipped out with the crowd and circled ahead.

Chapter 22

Milan's freight yard stank of diesel and wet stone. They watched from the shadow of a low wall, breath fogging in the night.

Forklifts crawled under sodium lamps, arms lifting sealed containers and setting them down with mechanical care.

For two hours, the rhythm held. Then the crane swung a container from the flatbed and tilted it toward a squat concrete building. No one walked in alongside it. Whatever was inside wasn't meant to be seen.

Julian's hand tightened on the rail. He didn't speak until the zipper on Simon's bag rasped open.

"No," he breathed.

"Just a look," Simon said.

"With you, it's never just a look."

Simon ignored him. From the bag, he drew the recon unit: paperback-small, matte finish, rotors shrouded to blunt the sound. Experimental kit, passed to him in Royston's office with the suggestion it might prove useful —no serials, no paperwork, no proof it had ever existed.

The controller was blocky, with a monochrome LCD, stub antenna, and heavy toggles built for gloves. Spread-spectrum primary with a scratchy narrowband fallback. Cutting-edge for 1991—deniable eyes where none should exist.

He checked the wind, the lamps, the arc of the yard. Then he launched from the wall's shadow, keeping the machine low, skimming the fence line. The drone answered with a soft whine and a jittering feed on the handheld.

Cracked tarmac. A loading-bay lip. A forklift reversing. The driver wore a respirator, its straps glinting under light. The bay doors rolled up. For a breath, the feed showed inside the container.

Metal cages. A scrape. A low, constant tremor. Then eyeshine—too far apart, wrong for any animal Simon could name. The image stuttered, then slewed sideways.

"Pull it. Now," Julian hissed.

Simon yanked the stick. The feed tore—colour drained to ash, then snow. He killed the handheld by reflex. For a second, he stood with the cool plastic in his palm, chest tight, as if the sight still hovered in the air.

"They're dumping noise across the band—wide, deliberate."

"Which means they know," Julian answered.

A siren wound up inside the building—low at first, then sharp. Floodlights ignited, transforming the fog into white haze. The yard became an operating theatre. Men moved with sudden purpose. Gates clanged. Footsteps hammered concrete.

Simon slid the unit back into the bag with hands steady only by will. The handheld's link light blinked once, then went dark—like a breath cut short.

"Move," Julian said.

They dropped from the wall and hugged the building, wet stone biting their palms. They ran in bursts, cutting through alleys and traffic, the city swallowing them. Behind them, searchlights swept the perimeter, Italian voices barking through radios, clipped and urgent.

By the time they reached a tram shelter, the city noise had drowned the chase. Simon powered the handheld again. The screen showed nothing—no feed, no flight path, no record at all. The log had been erased, or taken.

He pulled his coat tighter, lungs burning. The cages hadn't been a glimpse—they were a summons. Whatever was inside wasn't meant to be seen, and now someone knew they had.

Chapter 23

The siren cut through Milan stone, metallic and cold. They broke from the yard's shadow, the city splintering into lanes and angles as they ran. Streetlamps hummed; arcs of light trembled on wet pavement.

"Two minutes before they're in the streets," Julian said. "Less if city police are on speed dial."

They folded into foot traffic—late workers, students under umbrellas, a woman dragging groceries. Simon kept his head down, the handheld tight in his grip. At a tram shelter, he risked a glance. The drone's last burst had tagged their position—enough for triangulation.

"They've got our grid."

"Then we hand them a decoy."

Julian steered him into a market square and toward a row of taxis. They climbed into the middle one. Julian gave a hotel across town in clipped Italian. The cab pulled away, wipers smearing neon across the windscreen. Two blocks later, they slipped out and into a delivery van idling in an alley. The driver, eyes forward, owed Julian a passport run in '89. He didn't greet them, didn't question —just eased the van back into traffic.

Back at the tram stop, a tall shadow slowed, radio at his collar.

"Control, confirm: target in sight. Orders?"

Static. Then: "Observe only. Not yet."

The words chilled more than the pursuit. "Not yet" meant planning, not mercy.

On the wall behind the tram shelter, paint peeled around a slogan: NESSUNO VEDE. Nobody sees. Simon read it twice, as if the wall itself was warning them.

The van rattled east toward the autostrada. By the time the facility's team reached the bogus hotel, Simon and Julian were already at Centrale, moving fast among travellers and night workers. Loudspeakers crackled departures in Italian and English, German names flattened by static. The concourse smelled of coffee gone bitter in urns.

They bought second-class tickets in cash, then slipped through the barriers. Simon snapped the handheld's RF module from its mount and fed the pieces into separate bins along the platform. Each clatter into the bin felt final, like shutting a door.

Onboard, the train lurched forward.

Outside, streetlamps burned a dull orange across the glass as Milan receded—arches, cranes, the faint silhouette of the Duomo spire swallowed by rain.

"We're not going back to Milan," Julian said low.

Simon leaned against the rattling window. "We don't need to. The next station's already on the line."

Chapter 24

Vienna was clean and cold; late-night streets gleamed from rain. They booked into a Pensione off Mariahilfer Straße—lace curtains, rotary phones, wallpaper the colour of old mustard. The receptionist slid a brass key across the counter without looking up.

Their room was narrow: two single beds, a radiator ticking in the corner, and a radio bolted to the wall. Outside, a tram rattled past, its wheels shrieking on wet rail. Somewhere in the city, bells tolled midnight.

Julian lit a Memphis beneath the no-smoking sign. Smoke curled against the glass, faint enough not to reach the corridor. He leaned on the sill, face drawn in the amber wash of a streetlamp. Somewhere below, a payphone rang twice and stopped, swallowed by rain.

"You can't keep doing this," he said.

"Doing what?"

"Dragging us across half of Europe with no plan for what happens if you're right."

The cages replayed behind Simon's eyes—bars slick with condensation, movement in the dark, wrong for freight.

"If I'm right," he said, voice low, "we've already seen enough."

Julian shook his head. "You treat this like code—crack it, move on. This isn't lines you can patch. It's lives. Once you open it, you don't shut it again."

Rain tapped the sill. A tram bell clanged; the U-Bahn groaned below, carrying night workers into tunnels. Vienna's streets, orderly and bright, offered no sign of freight yards or cages. That dissonance pressed harder than the cold.

Later, hunched in the hallway with the phone and acoustic coupler, Simon scrolled a Usenet feed. The modem hissed and sputtered against the handset. Lines of text crept across the monochrome screen—fragments, chatter, junk. Then a phrase snagged his eye. No name, but the cadence was there: blunt, clipped, precise. Sophie's cadence. She was out there, somewhere, pulling threads. The silence felt less complete.

For a moment, he thought of Royston—his scrawled notes, the case unlocked in his office, the kit he'd all but pressed into Simon's hands. Maybe Sophie was leaving her own trail, threading fragments into a pattern he was meant to see.

Back in the room, Julian sat with his back to the radiator, cigarette stubbed out in a saucer. He watched Simon for a long moment, eyes narrowed, unreadable. The glance carried want, quickly buried beneath control.

"There's someone here I trust," Julian said at last. "An academic. Knows the yards and the ministries. He can get us closer without another siren."

"Old friend?" Simon asked.

"Something like that."

The words lingered, heavier than they should. Simon didn't press.

They switched off the lamp. Rain streaked the window; tram wheels hissed past. The pensione's thin walls carried muffled radios, a laugh, the clink of bottles. Normal life continued, steady, ignorant.

Simon lay awake, the hum from Milan still in his bones.

Every possibility has owners, Sophie had said. In Vienna, the truth pressed sharper—closer. He shut his eyes, but the cages came with him into the dark.

Chapter 25

They walked east through narrowing streets until shops gave way to older blocks. Julian stopped at a once-blue building, dulled to grey, and pressed the buzzer twice.

"Julian?" A warm male voice crackled through the intercom.

"Yeah. Been a while."

The lock buzzed. The man who opened the door was tall, sharp-featured, in a charcoal jumper. Surprise shifted into warmth.

"Christ — it has been a while." He pulled Julian into a brief embrace that lingered half a second too long.

"This is Simon," Julian said. "We need a quiet word."

Inside, the flat smelled of books and stale wine. Shelves bowed under paperbacks; a radio hummed low. Against one stack leaned a photograph: Julian younger, arm slung around Markus in summer light.

Markus poured wine into three chipped glasses and sat opposite, measuring Simon with the calm of a man who made his living weighing risk.

"We're tracking a shipment out of Milan," Julian said. "Biological cargo. You still have friends in the yards?"

"Some," Markus said. "Enough to ask the wrong questions without losing my job. And if I say no?"

"Then we find someone else," Simon said. "But we don't stop."

Markus refilled the glasses. "You've learned bluntness. Good." He paused, studying Julian. "But you should be careful. Men like the ones who ran you don't retire. They just change desks. Different titles, same work. You know that better than most."

Julian's features tightened but he said nothing. The room cooled. Outside, a tram bell clanged against the rain.

"I'll try Verona," Markus went on. "There's a team that runs the freight lanes. If they talk, we'll know how the trucks clear the borders. But remember—when you wake people like this, they don't always go back to sleep."

The plan folded like a map. They drank. They waited. Vienna carried its low mechanical pulse beyond the glass, trams groaning, rain tapping the sill.

Julian smoked in silence, gaze fixed on the window. Markus refilled the glasses slowly, as if weighing risk with each pour. Simon leafed through the papers, every shuffle whispering back the same images: cages in Milan, the hum under the forest, Sophie's clipped cadence threaded through places it shouldn't be. None of it let him rest.

For a moment, it felt almost safe—three men in a cluttered room, wine dark in the glasses, city noise muffled beyond the curtains. But the quiet carried weight, as if the past was sitting at the table too, uninvited and patient, breathing faintly between them.

Chapter 26

Pale light pressed through the lace curtains. Markus had been on the phone since dawn, his voice pitched low, German softened by bureaucratic French. He paced as he spoke, hand braced against the glass as though the rain outside might shield him.

When he finally hung up, he turned back to them, shoulders drawn.

"Verona," he said. "The cargo switches there—onto trucks cleared for pharma. Pallets sealed as vaccines. When necessary, they move under diplomatic cover."

Julian leaned forward, brow creased. "Which ministry signs?"

Markus shook his head. "That's above my reach. The routing is protected. But the trucks don't go south, not to Rome. They go east. Toward Trieste."

Simon looked up sharply. "Trieste puts them on the Adriatic."

"Exactly," Markus said. "From there, they vanish."

The words hung in the small room. Simon thought of the cages in Milan, breath caught behind mesh, the scrape inside steel. He wondered what could be hidden in pallets marked for vaccines—what weight could vanish so easily under a false seal.

Markus poured coffee, but his hands weren't steady. The cups clinked too hard against the saucers. "You shouldn't follow this line," he said. "It doesn't end."

Julian's reply was almost a whisper. "It ends for someone."

Markus's eyes flicked to him, holding a trace of reproach. "Still the same. Always certain, even when the ground moves under you."

Julian didn't answer. His features tightened, silence a wall he pulled up between them.

Outside, tram wheels hissed on wet track. Vienna carried its usual calm—trams, radios, the hum of the U-Bahn below—but Simon heard only the echo of the pines. Ammonia sharp. Machinery constant. The hum that seemed to follow them across borders.

Markus lingered by the door, palm against the frame as though steadying himself. His voice, when it came, was quiet but final. "Be careful. Men who can move freight under diplomatic plates don't forgive. They don't forget. And they don't sleep once you wake them."

Julian gave a short nod, nothing more. But Simon noticed the way Markus's gaze caught on him—an old familiarity sharpened into something like accusation. Whatever history bound them, it hadn't gentled with time.

Julian tucked the folded papers inside his coat. Simon saw Markus's eyes follow the gesture—papers heavy with risk, but also with direction.

Rain mottled the pavement as they stepped outside. The air was sharp, almost metallic. Simon hunched into his jacket, but Julian walked with his head high, as if defiance alone could keep the city from pressing down.

Vienna held its silence. But the papers in Julian's coat bent east, pulling them toward the next crossing.

Graz was next.

Chapter 27

The road east from Graz was slick with last night's rain. They'd traded trains for a rented Peugeot, its dull paint and boxy lines blending into border traffic. No one would remember it. That was the point.

Two car lengths ahead, the Hungarian-plated truck kept a steady pace. The container was the same faded green— anonymous but for a stencilled code in chipped paint. To anyone else, it was freight in the tide of Europe's rebuilding. To Simon, it was the thread they couldn't drop.

Julian unfolded a Michelin map across his knees, biro circling a thin red line through border towns.

"They'll hit Szentgotthárd in twenty minutes. Across that barrier, it's a different game. New guards. New rules."

Simon kept his hands loose on the wheel. "Then we stay in this one until it's done."

Rain streaked the windscreen. At the border, traffic bunched into queues under humming lamps. Trabants and Ladas coughed blue exhaust into the drizzle. A battered bus idled in line, children pressed to its fogged windows while their teacher argued with a guard in a peaked cap. The man barely glanced at her documents, his expression one of practised indifference.

Another officer leaned against a prefab hut, cigarette ember glowing. His eyes only lifted when the truck rolled past. A nod, a flick of the hand. Waved through without inspection.

The Peugeot crawled forward. A clipboard rested under the guard's arm, rain sliding across its plastic sleeve. Julian's voice was low, steady, rehearsed.

"Your turn."

Simon reached under the seat, pulling out a second set of plates. Austrian diplomatic paperwork, Markus had insisted, was too much risk. They snapped into place with a muted click. He slid his passport across, the laminate cool against his fingers.

The guard's thumb lingered at the edge. His gaze flicked up, weighing both faces. Julian's still, Simon's unreadable. The pause stretched until sweat pooled at Simon's collar.

Then the barrier lifted.

Two minutes later, they were over the line, tyres humming on Hungarian asphalt. The truck was still ahead, taillights a dull red glow in the mist.

The landscape opened into flat fields, poplars lining the road like mute sentries. Roadside shrines appeared in the beams—whitewashed niches, saints watching over wet ground, candles guttering in jars.

Julian exhaled slowly, almost a laugh. "We just committed an international crime."

"Add it to the list," Simon said, eyes fixed on the truck.

The wipers beat in rhythm. Border lights receded in the rear-view, swallowed by fog. Ahead, Hungary stretched flat and grey, the road pulling them deeper east.

The game hadn't changed. Only the ground beneath it.

Chapter 28

The flat sat above a shuttered bakery, the smell of yeast clinging even at night. Markus had arranged it—cash only, no register, no questions. A single bulb dangled from the ceiling; the plaster walls were streaked with damp. From the window, they had a line on the road a block away.

The truck had passed twenty minutes earlier, heading southeast. At a petrol stop near the crossing, Simon had crouched low and fixed a magnetic tracker beneath the chassis—a resin pebble disguised as road grit. Now its pulse blinked across the handheld, faint and imperfect, each blip like a heartbeat. The unit was the same Royston had pressed into his hands in Cambridge, its screen dim, its toggles heavy, built for field use.

Julian spread Markus's papers across the table, corners pinned with a chipped ashtray.

"Diplomatic plates mean clearance," he said. "The question is—destination or handoff?"

"At this pace, Kecskemét by dawn," Simon answered.

"And then?"

"Then we see if it's money, politics…" He hesitated. "Or worse."

The silence stretched. A motorbike droned into the lane, engine note deepening as it slowed. They both moved to the window.

The rider stopped directly below. Helmet black, visor down. A gloved hand rose and tapped once against the glass—slow, deliberate. Not a wave. Not impatience. An acknowledgement.

Julian's breath fogged the pane. A hiss of radio leaked as the rider shifted. The head tilted back, gaze fixed upward. After a beat too long, the engine revved. The bike rolled on, growl fading in measured rhythm, as though counting their stay.

A dog barked once in the next courtyard, then cut off mid-note. The bakery walls held the quiet.

"Could be nothing," Simon said, though his hand hovered near the satchel with the picks and the pistol. Julian didn't move from the window. "No one follows us this far by accident."

They watched until the red taillight curved out of sight. The sound lingered longer, echoing off narrow streets.

Simon rechecked the handheld. The tracker's pulse glowed steady, a dim green dot crawling southeast. He felt the urge to anchor himself to it—the one constant, the one thread he could hold.

Julian turned from the glass at last. "We move at dawn. Stay ahead of the truck, not behind it."

Simon nodded, but his eyes stayed on the tracker's glow.

Steady. Small. Alive.

Chapter 29

For a moment, Simon heard Sophie's voice—*rules only bend until they finally snap*. He couldn't place the memory exactly. Frost on the Cambridge lawn, her scarf wrapped to her chin, words half-lost in breath—or maybe his own mind stitching her cadence into what he needed to hear now. Either way, it surfaced, sharp and unwelcome.

By first light, the tracker's pulse had drawn them southeast, across flat fields and railway cuts, into the sprawl of Kecskemét. The town smelled faintly of jet fuel from the nearby airbase, a tang that clung to the mist.

The Hungarian-plated truck did not head for the gates. Instead, it turned off the main road toward a tired industrial park, relics of another decade. The guard hut sagged under a corrugated roof, its windows patched with yellowing tape. Chain-link fences sagged too, reinforced with scrap panels stencilled in Cyrillic. Beyond, grey blocks of workers' flats loomed, stairwells leaking radio noise—snatches of Vienna pop colliding with Moscow bulletins.

Simon parked the Peugeot in the shadows two streets away, tucking it between rusting containers and a burned-out Lada. They moved the rest on foot, breath clouding in the morning chill. A gap in the fence, half-torn by weather, let them slip inside. Asphalt glistened with thin rain, reflecting the lamps overhead.

The truck idled beside a corrugated warehouse, its engine ticking as it cooled. No one moved to unload it. Two men lounged against the bumper, uniforms thrown together from surplus fatigues. No insignia. No rank. But the boots were American—too new, too clean—and the cigarettes lit between their fingers weren't local stock. Not conscripts. Not the army. Contractors. Outsiders.

Simon didn't answer. His focus was on the warehouse.

At the far side, a loading dock gaped, shutter raised just enough to slice the dark. Light cut a strip across stacked cages—identical to Milan. Bars slick with condensation.

Shapes pressed at them—pale, restless, scraping metal into sound. Panic given form, stripped of words, stripped of sense.

Julian's jaw locked. His whisper came strained. "We're out of time."

Simon's reply was flat, colder than the air. "No. We're exactly on it."

A cigarette ember arced across the tarmac, tossed carelessly. It hissed in the wet. Both men dropped back, slipping through the fence.

The street beyond felt too open, silence heavier than engines and radios behind them.

Every possibility has owners.

The words were Sophie's—or maybe now he owned them. Either way, they rang the same.

Chapter 30

Julian stirred his coffee. "You realise you're suggesting we break into a secure site in a NATO country."

"I realise we may have proof of something no one wants exposed," Simon said. "That cargo won't stay. Once it moves, we've lost it."

"And if it's guarded the way I think it is," Julian said, "we may never walk out."

Simon leaned over the paper map on the table, finger pressing to a pencilled mark. "Here. The fencing is thinner. Fewer sightlines. They're running passive sensors —trip beams, heat triggers. I can give us a gap. Not long, but enough to see what's inside."

Julian's stare was level. "You're talking about stepping into a place no one is meant to leave."

Simon didn't answer.

The silence stretched, broken only by the drip of a leaking tap. At last, Julian exhaled. "One hour after nightfall. No heroics."

"No promises," Simon said.

―――

Moonlight pooled in rain-slick puddles. Dark clothes, gloves, nothing they couldn't drop. Floodlights fractured across the yard in cold arcs.

At the north wall, Simon crouched by the fence. The transmitter's LED blinked red in his palm.

"Once I start this, six minutes," he said.

Julian's reply was flat. "Make them count."

The fence groaned as Simon clipped the bypass. Red flicked to green. They slipped inside.

The warehouse loomed, corrugated flanks sweating condensation. Even outside, the air hit them—chemical, raw. Formaldehyde laced with disinfectant, sharp enough to burn the nose. Not hospital clean, but a crude, industrial parody.

Tarps lined the concrete floor, edges damp, pooling condensation into dark patches. Shapes lay beneath them—too even, too still for freight. The air carried something else now, under the chemicals: breath, faint and wrong, like exhalations forced through cloth.

Simon crouched, hand hovering before it settled on a corner. He peeled the tarp back an inch. Then another.

Not cargo. Not crates.

A face looked out—small, pale, eyes wide but hollow, too steady to belong in a place like this. Fingers pressed white against mesh, knuckles strained, the sound behind them a muffled chorus of scraping metal and stifled panic.

Julian's hand clamped his shoulder, iron tight. His jaw worked but no words came.

Then a voice rose from deeper in the dark—low, precise, recited like ledger entries:

"Don't mistake the function. Silence comes cheaper when bought young. Officials look away more easily when their ledgers are already dirty."

A figure stepped into half-light, clipboard under one arm, coat cut sharp, gait military. The tone was bureaucratic, detached—like cargo weights spoken aloud.

The words pressed heavier than the stench. Julian's eyes flickered once toward the figure—recognition he buried as fast as it surfaced.

Boots struck concrete deeper in the warehouse, deliberate and closing. Torches flared along the inner walls, beams slicing through the tarps. The transmitter in Simon's pocket blinked from green to amber.

Julian hissed, urgent: "We go. Now."

Simon dropped the tarp, sealing the face in shadow again. They moved low, fast, slipping between stacks until the exit gaped ahead.

A searchlight swept the yard as they cleared the fence, beams chasing but not catching.

Outside, the night offered no relief. The chemical tang clung to their throats, soaked into their skin.

Behind them, the tarps swallowed the cages.

The transmitter died in Simon's hand, LED fading to black.

They ran until the city swallowed them.

Chapter 31

They didn't stop until the flat above the bakery in Szombathely. Simon went straight to the sink, twisting the cold tap, sluicing water over his face until it ran down his sleeves. His hands still shook. Even scrubbed raw, the faint tang of varnish clung to his skin.

Julian locked the door and drew the curtains tight. The room was spare: a table, two chairs, a coil heater in the corner. The smell of yeast drifted up from the ovens below, too ordinary against what they'd seen.

"Talk," Julian said.

Simon leaned over the basin. His voice caught, then steadied. "Children. They're moving children."

Julian's eyes dropped to the manifests on the table. He lifted the top sheet as if to check it, but his thumb snagged something folded small beneath—an unsigned addendum, edges worn soft. His gaze lingered too long; the colour drained from his face before he forced it back. He slipped the paper into his coat, hand resting against the lining, protective, almost possessive.

Simon saw, and chose not to speak.

Julian tapped the pile instead. "We can't take this to the police. Not here. Not now. You saw the plates, the guards. This runs higher."

"Then we leak it," Simon said. "I can scatter the manifests, routing notes, scraps from Milan across a dozen servers in an hour."

"And then what?" Julian's tone sharpened. "They scrub the logs, move the cargo, bury the story. You don't win by shouting into the void. This has to be handled quietly."

"You sound like Royston," Simon muttered.
Julian's head snapped up, eyes hard. "If you want them freed, the story matters more than the facts. The wrong story buries them faster than a grave."

Simon gripped the sink. Sophie's words—every possibility has owners—slid through his head. Less a warning now, more a manual.

He dropped into a chair. The table was cold beneath his arms. From below, a brass tune leaked through the floorboards, warped and homely. Life carried on as though cages had never existed.

Julian sat opposite, expression flat. "I'll call someone I trust. Promise me—no freelance heroics."

"You know I can't promise that."

The heater clicked. Rain tapped the shutters. The smell of bread thickened, clashing with memory.

Simon stared at his damp hands until they steadied. But the image stayed: a pale face at mesh, knuckles white, a mouth opening without sound.

Julian met his eyes, the lapse gone. His voice was controlled again. "Pack. If they come, we move before they knock."

Simon's jaw clenched. He slid the laptop into its case, checked the floppies in his jacket pocket. From below, trays clanged as bakers set dough into ovens. The smell of yeast thickened the air. Too ordinary.

"We need more than words," Simon said. "Proof they can't bury. Something physical. Images. Files. Otherwise, they'll vanish everything—including us."

Julian didn't argue. His silence was agreement. He only said, "Then all lines stay dead. No calls. No uploads. Not until we have something they can't scrub."

Simon glanced at the dark laptop, its dull casing reflecting nothing. "Then we move quietly. Hard evidence, not chatter."

Outside, a car door thudded. Then another. Voices carried low, blurred by rain.

Neither man spoke. The air held still, heavy with yeast and the chemical stench still clinging to their clothes.

Julian stepped to the door, voice low, deliberate.

"Quiet."

Simon didn't answer. The word lodged anyway.

Rain pressed harder against the shutters, as if the city itself was holding its breath for what came next.

Chapter 33

Simon edged the curtain aside. A black van idled at the corner, lights off, exhaust breathing white into the rain.

"They found us," Julian said, pulling on his boots.

They worked fast. Papers swept into bags, manifests folded tight. Simon flipped the Compaq LTE open one last time. The screen glowed dim, a green cursor blinking like a pulse. He shut down clean, yanked the modem lead, and palmed the floppies into his jacket. The laptop itself was too heavy, too rare. He pulled the hard drive—slab the size of a pack of cards—and slid it into the lining of his coat.

As the screen faded, a hidden login flickered red once—flagged, quarantined, not erased. Someone had seen it, considered, and left it alive. Mercy—or bait.

Van doors thudded. Two men stepped out, coats dark, breath clouding in the cold. One swept a wand along the bakery wall, deliberate, methodical.

"Rear stairwell. Quiet," Julian said.

They slipped into the corridor behind the ovens. The air was thick with flour and old heat. Simon's boots skidded on the tiles, breath catching in the stifling mix of yeast and steam. Julian guided him to the back, easing the door open without a sound.

The alley lay damp and narrow, walls weeping condensation. At the far end, Simon risked a glance back. One of the men stood directly beneath their window, head tilted, listening as if the bricks themselves might confess.

Julian's whisper cut the air. "If they're here to talk, I don't want to hear it. If they're here to kill us—we're already gone."

They moved fast, pressed tight to the wall. Rain slicked their shoulders, pooled around broken cobbles. Behind them, the bakery's front door creaked open. Hinges moaned—loud as a shout in the morning quiet. For a heartbeat, Simon thought he heard their names in the sound.

They didn't run, not yet. Running drew eyes. They walked with purpose, cutting into the warren of streets where laundry lines sagged across alleys and shuttered stalls glistened with rain.

Simon forced himself not to look back. Every footstep echoed too sharply, every streetlamp hummed too long. The city felt watchful, like glass held to the skin.

The van remained out of sight, but the sense of pursuit clung—silent, patient, waiting for them to turn the wrong corner.

Simon kept his eyes on the wet stone ahead. The doubt gnawed anyway: he couldn't tell if Julian was pulling him away from danger—or straight toward it.

Chapter 34

They caught a local train before sunrise, the kind that stopped at every siding. The carriage smelled of old smoke and rain trapped in cloth. Simon kept his face to the window, watching fields roll past in half-light. Commuters dozed behind newspapers, briefcases on their knees, umbrellas dripping into the aisle.

Two stops later, they stepped down onto the platform. No announcements, just a loudspeaker crackling with static. They crossed the tracks and cut into the fields. Frost clung to the sleepers; the air was raw enough to bite the lungs. Each sound—dogs barking in the distance, the crunch of their boots—felt magnified.

Julian kept a folded Michelin map in his coat pocket, worn soft at the creases. No signals, no calls, no traces. By the canal, he stopped, opened it across his knee, and smoothed the line with deliberate care.

"East," he said. "There's a farmhouse eight kilometres out. Empty most of the year."

Simon glanced at him. "Yours?"

"A friend's," Julian said. His tone carried no detail. "The kind who doesn't ask."

They walked without speaking. Crows scattered from stubble fields. Water pooled black in the ruts. Simon found himself counting steps, as if the numbers might hold the silence back.

By mid-morning, the farmhouse rose ahead: shutters crooked, timber warped, a pump rusting by the well. No smoke, no sound. The sort of place that might vanish if you looked away too long.

Inside, plaster flaked in sheets. Wallpaper bubbled, floorboards sagged but held. Julian moved through each room with soldier's caution—corners, windows, doors. He lingered a fraction too long at the thresholds, listening to the silences as if they could betray him, then dropped his bag on the kitchen table.

Simon stayed at the cracked window with his notebook open. Routes and numbers traced in pencil, arrows threading across the page. Some lines ran clean, others veered east into gaps where nothing was marked—spaces that shouldn't have been blank. He pressed harder with the pencil, forcing a line into absence. The pattern was incomplete, but the weight behind it wasn't. He saw what the paper couldn't hold: faces pressed to mesh, small hands clinging until the knuckles whitened.

At the table, Julian unfolded the map again, smoothing the crease flat. His fingers brushed his coat pocket—where the folded addendum lay—as if by accident. Too careful for chance. Simon saw it, registered the gesture, but left it unspoken.

The farmhouse held still. Outside, the wind rattled the shutters.

Chapter 35

No power. Damp walls. The faint reek of varnish.

Simon cleared the kitchen table, set down the black case, and pulled out the laptop. Blocky, dull grey, LCD the colour of weak tea. He wired it into a portable battery pack meant for field radios. In Milan and Dordrecht, there had been sockets, adapters, ways to steal current. Here, there was nothing but plaster and silence. The pack would give him half an hour at best.

Julian leaned in the doorway. "We agreed—no connections."

"We agreed—no stupidity," Simon said. "Thirty in, thirty out."

The machine gave a thin whine. The screen blinked to life, green code spooling like rain. Static chewed the edges, then steadied. Simon's pulse lifted with the signal.

Simon keyed through the buried threads on the Tallinn server—fragments he suspected Sophie had planted, her cadence hidden in verdicts and clauses. It was enough to follow the ghost trails she'd left behind, leading him to the data she'd managed to upload.

The screen shifted. A crude still image resolved, blocky but intact. Rows of cages. Tarps half-pulled back. Condensation beading against the mesh. Faces behind the bars—children, eyes glass-bright, reflecting strip light.

Simon froze, breath shallow.

Behind the cages, a man moved across the frame. Charcoal coat. Clipboard under one arm. Square shoulders, military in posture, even without insignia. The grain was harsh, the angle poor—but it held.

Julian's hand shot to the doorframe, grip white. He stared at the screen, hollow, as though he'd been waiting for this image his whole life.

"I know him," he breathed.

Simon turned slowly. "Then tell me why he's moving children."

Julian's jaw worked. For a moment, he said nothing. When the words came, they cracked.

"Carter." The name seemed to choke him. "He was in the ledger—my father's, Royston's. I saw it once. His name, then struck through in green. That was how they erased people. No record, no trail. Scrubbed so no one ever asked who gave them orders."

He shook his head, breath catching. "I thought he'd been buried. That was the only mercy I believed in."

The silence pressed between them, heavier than the damp walls.

"But he's here."

Simon looked back at the frozen frame: the cages, the pale faces, Carter pacing with a clipboard as if logging cargo weights.

Julian's voice was low, ragged. "If Carter still exists, then the worst of it was true. And I was never meant to walk free either."

The battery ticked faintly in its cradle. Simon shut the lid, but the image lingered between them, burned into the air.

CHAPTER 36

The farmhouse held its silence. Wind needled at the shutters, rattling them with every gust.

The laptop lay shut on the counter, but the image lingered in the room: a man in a charcoal coat, hair clipped close, clipboard tucked under his arm.

Julian sat at the kitchen table, elbows set, head slightly bowed. When he spoke, the words seemed weighed against something he didn't want to let surface.

"Carter. He started in uniform—in places you never read about. Counter-insurgency, advisory cadres, the kind of postings you're not supposed to admit exist. When he left, he wasn't discarded. He was picked up."

Simon leaned against the cracked window. "By who?"

"Front companies. Private contracts. Call it security." Julian's jaw tightened on the word. "Royston trusted men like him. They carried what couldn't exist—money, weapons, people. All deniable." His fingers smoothed the table's scarred wood, an unconscious motion repeated until it became deliberate. "Last time I heard, Carter was in the Gulf. Then he vanished. The ledger marked him struck through. I thought that meant erased."

He paused, knuckles whitening where his hand pressed into the table. For a moment, his gaze dropped, fixed on the wood as though the grain itself might open a way out. When he looked up, the mask slipped: his voice thinned, rough at the edges.

"But he's here. Running cages."

Simon exhaled hard, the weight of the admission settling. "Then we follow him."

Julian's mouth moved before sound came. "Do you understand what that means? Once you follow Carter, you're not chasing a man. You're stepping onto a board built to consume you. And once you're on it, there's no stepping off."

"You talk about boards like I've ever had a place on one," Simon said. "My uncle died in Belfast because someone higher up moved pieces he never saw. I don't care about their game. I care about those children."

Julian made a sound—short, breathless, almost a laugh, but strangled. His hand lifted, hovered, then smoothed the table again, harder this time, as though ironing something that couldn't be made flat. His tone dropped, quieter, unwilling but true.

"Then care about staying alive long enough to matter."

He rose slowly, shoulders drawn, and brushed Simon's arm as he passed. The contact was steady but fleeting, too purposeful to be an accident. Simon watched him move to the window.

Julian's reflection in the glass looked hollowed—haunted by more than Carter's name.

The farmhouse groaned with the wind. Outside, the shutters rattled again, restless, as though even the walls recognised the weight Carter carried back into the world.

Chapter 37

Two days later, they saw him.

Carter stepped from a government building in Székesfehérvár, a cigarette already burning between his fingers. He walked at an unhurried pace — men like him never rushed. Their gait told the world they had nothing to fear.

The Lada had come from one of Markus's contacts — cash only, no questions. The heater barely worked, but forgettable was the point. Oil and old cloth clung to the seats. Julian kept one hand on the wheel, the other loose near the gearstick, eyes fixed on Carter.

"Rule one of a tail," he murmured. "Stay boring. Don't give him a reason to remember you."

Simon scanned the street, noting CCTV placements, already calculating which feeds he might ghost later. "I'll take boring over dead."

Carter flicked his cigarette into the gutter and slid into a dark SUV. They followed at a distance, letting traffic swallow their presence. The route wound past shuttered factories and hollow housing blocks until the SUV slowed and turned into a rail yard.

Through the fence, they saw him speaking with a man in a tailored coat, silver watch-face flashing.

Julian's eyes narrowed — not just recognition, but calculation. Caldwell had worn the same style once, years ago. Royston's circle had tastes that bled together: money, power, silence dressed in tailored cloth.

A crane groaned overhead, lowering a container onto a flatbed. Chains rattled, padlocks clamped tight. Simon's gut clenched. He recognised the locks — the same design as in the warehouse, the same that held cages. Faces pressed against the wire flickered unbidden in his mind.

Julian's voice was low. "That's our trail."

Simon's reply was tight, almost a vow. "And we're not losing it."

Pinned to a shed wall, a manifest flapped in the wind. Two columns ran side by side: sensitive assets and special cargo. No line between them. Human lives and hardware, balanced in the same ink. Simon's throat tightened. To Carter's world, there was no difference.

Carter turned back toward his SUV. He paused mid-step, the cigarette ember still glowing faintly at his side. His gaze swept the yard, but not like a man checking the perimeter. Slower. More deliberate. His head tilted, eyes tracking along the fence line until they stopped exactly where Simon crouched in the shadows.

For a heartbeat, Simon's lungs refused air. His body locked under Carter's stare — not surprise, not confusion, but recognition. The kind that said I see you. I expected you. And I'm letting you know.

Then Carter smiled. Thin. Knowing. He tapped ash to the ground, climbed into the SUV, and shut the door. The slam echoed like a verdict.

Chapter 38

They waited in the dark until Carter's SUV rolled toward the gate. He didn't hurry. He never did. At the checkpoint, he paused, window sliding down, exchanging a few words with the guard. His hand gestured once — sharp, dismissive — and the barrier lifted.

For a moment, the SUV idled. Carter's head turned slightly, eyes sweeping the yard as though taking inventory. The beam of a lamp caught the hard line of his profile, unblinking. Even from a distance, Simon felt it — not a glance, not a search, but a deliberate look into shadow. His chest locked. It wasn't surprise in Carter's face. It was recognition. The kind that said I see you. I expected you. And I'm letting you know.

Then the gears engaged, the SUV eased forward, and the gate clanged shut behind him. The echo lingered long after the tyres had gone.

Only then did they move. The night was knife-sharp, sodium lamps spilling fractured pools of orange across the tracks. Every step on the gravel sounded too loud, too final.

The container loomed on the flatbed, chained and padlocked, steel sweating in the cold. Simon crouched at the undercarriage, pulse hammering. From his bag he drew the tracker — palm-sized, wires hand-soldered, casing dulled with grit. The magnets snapped hard against the steel, the sound clanging through his chest like a gunshot.

He froze. No alarm. No shout. Only the groan of a shunt engine starting, iron grinding against iron as though the yard itself had heard him.

Julian's whisper was taut. "Three minutes. No more."

Simon flicked the switch. The LED blinked once, steady and green — a tiny heartbeat pulsing against the dark. Behind the locked doors he imagined knuckles whitening against mesh, breath held as tightly as his own.

A searchlight beam swept the gravel, skimming so close it lit the sweat on Julian's cheek before drifting away. Both men stayed rigid until the glare moved on.

"Done," Simon breathed.

Julian didn't look back. His voice came clipped, almost mechanical. "Then we're ghosts." As he spoke, he tugged his cuff straight, aligning the fabric too carefully, the gesture sharp with restraint.

Simon saw it — the same ritual precision as with the napkin. A tell he hadn't meant to notice, but now couldn't unsee. Julian's mask was intact, but the edges strained.

They slipped into the lamp-broken dark, chains clanking and engines rumbling behind them, the yard stirring awake as if it knew something had been left behind.

Chapter 39

Back at the farmhouse, a pulsing dot crawled across Simon's portable monitor, following the rails west.

"Heading for Austria," Julian murmured.

"If it crosses the border, we lose it in hours," Simon said. He couldn't take his eyes off the light. To him, it wasn't a signal — it was cages in motion, faces jolted with every mile.

Julian paced. "Car's too slow to follow by rail."

"Then we beat it there."

By morning, they were on backroads shadowing the line. At Sopron, the tracker showed the train slowing. Julian pulled up on a hill, binoculars steady.

"There. Same container. They're coupling it to a faster freight."

Simon frowned. "You know what chasing this means."

Julian smiled thinly. "Good. Maybe we'll finally see who's paying him."

They crossed into Czechia after midnight, no checkpoint, just a faded sign and the tarmac changing under their wheels. Headlights smeared across the wet road.

Simon checked the feed. "Stopped outside Brno. Transfer point, maybe."

From a ridge, they saw warehouses and a rail spur under sickly orange lights. Chains rattled, echoing across the yard. Once, Simon thought he heard a muffled cry — high, thin, carried by the wind — and his stomach twisted.

Julian killed the engine. "If they're unloading here, Carter's handing off."

Simon scanned the fence. "Thinking of going in?"

Julian's look was enough. "First, we see who he's meeting."

Two trucks reversed into the shed. The men moved like soldiers, civilian clothes hiding drilled discipline.

"Not locals," Julian whispered. "These are pros."

A door at the far end opened. A figure stepped into the light, coat collar turned high against the cold. For a moment, Carter stood framed in sodium orange — and then another silhouette followed.

Simon didn't recognise him. Julian did. His breath caught, voice dropping to almost nothing.

"Caldwell."

The name hit like a stone. Simon remembered it from the ledgers: a backbench MP disgraced years earlier for undeclared defence interests. The £38,400 transfer in 1991, the breakfast headline on his uncle's table. Supposedly finished.

Yet here he was, signing manifests beside Carter, treating cages like line items. For a second, Caldwell's composure slipped — the pen shook between his fingers before he steadied it, jaw tightening as if willing the tremor away.

Julian's breath caught, not just with fury but with the memory of a boy who had once wanted men, before learning what wanting cost. The shame flickered and was gone, replaced by ice.

His whisper was flat, taut. "He was never finished. He was promoted."

He didn't say more. His jaw locked, hands tightening on the binoculars until his knuckles whitened. For a heartbeat, Simon thought he saw something else flicker across his face — memory, recognition, maybe even shame — before the mask slid back into place.

"Now you see it," Julian said quietly. "This isn't contraband. It's statecraft."

Chapter 40

The Brno yard stank of diesel and damp iron. Sodium lamps smeared pale light across the gravel, throwing shadows twice their size. Every groan of machinery seemed amplified, each clang of chain a reminder of weight being shifted, not just steel.

From the ridge, Simon watched through the fence, breath shallow. The rail spur shuddered as a crane lowered a container, locks snapping shut with the dull certainty of routine. He didn't need to see inside to know what it carried. His gut already supplied the sound: knuckles against mesh, breaths stifled in cloth.

At the centre of the yard, Carter preferred silence. He didn't need speeches; the paper spoke. The manifest lay open on a crate lid, black ink drying neat and final. His initials were geometry — a curve, a line, a dot. No flourish. Authority without effort.

Beside him, Caldwell hunched deeper into his coat, breath fogging. His voice was low, uneasy. "Exposure?"

"Always," Carter said. Even, unhurried. "But never what matters." He folded the sheet with measured care. "Move the stock, balance the books. Numbers align."

Julian's grip tightened on the binoculars, knuckles white. Simon glanced sideways. There was recognition there — not just of Carter, but of the pattern, the cadence. Julian's face had gone still, too still, as if the sound of those words was a return he hadn't asked for.

"And the assets?" Caldwell pressed.

"Sound enough. Transit only. Intent lies elsewhere."

The crane groaned again, metal teeth biting. The yard seemed to bow under it. Carter didn't look. He already knew the locks. He passed the folder to a waiting handler — broad-shouldered, no adornment, the kind Royston's circle always picked when subtlety was cheaper than loyalty.

"Geneva first," Carter said. "Swiss paperwork, if anyone stares."

Simon felt Julian's breath hitch, just audible in the dark.

Then Carter turned his head. Slow. Deliberate. Not a sweep of the yard, not a man checking security. His eyes moved with the patience of someone cataloguing inventory. They found the fence line, the stillness too precise. Two figures in shadow, breath held.

He let his gaze rest, a half second longer than manners, then away. No signal to the guards. No raised voice. Recognition was enough.

At the SUV, Carter struck a match on his thumbnail, smoke curling into the sodium haze. The light caught his profile, hard, unblinking. A gift to the watchers: *I see you. I expected you. We will play by the rules if you understand them.*

The door slammed shut like a verdict. The convoy rolled out, engines low, carrying cages westward.

Behind the fence, Julian lowered the binoculars. His hands shook once before he stilled them flat against his knees.

Simon said nothing. Carter had already spoken enough for both of them.

Chapter 41

The motorway hummed under the tyres. Brno's glow thinned to dark country, then the clean geometry of Czech tarmac. Carter sat in silence with a notebook on his knee.

One minister, compliant.
Two handlers, competent.
One yard, adequate.
One container, sealed and tracked.
Two observers, hungry.

He wrote this beneath a column headed Friction. Opposition wasn't a flaw; it was a function. Auditors kept a system honest.

The secure handset pulsed in its cradle. A relay crackled, stretching the silence the way scramblers do. Then a man's voice came through, blurred by distance yet surgical in tone.

"Report."

"Hand-off complete," Carter said. "Line item seven-C enters Austrian ledger at zero-four-twenty. Transit friction: expected."

"Views?"

"Two. Milan again. Home-made equipment. Not State, but drilled."

A pop of static, then: "Action?"

"None. Let them learn."

Another pause moved along the wire, as if a listener had taken one step closer.

"Royston will want his page."

"He'll have it by breakfast."

The line clicked to a soft hum. Carter set the handset down with the same precision he afforded signatures.

Vienna rose from the dark like a model—trams, wires, façades arranged for the comfort of officials. He took the hotel room facing the Ringstraße and laid paper on the desk: heavy stock, watermark faint as breath. The Swan pen bled a clean, exact green.

— 7C reconciled.

— Minister briefed (Trade).

— Transit contracted with Swiss cover.

— Audit minor.

— Public phrase: humanitarian transfer.

— Private phrase: debts settled.

He did not write children. The word was imprecise. Children were not payment; payment was silence, leverage, continuity—entries that travelled cleanly to the next page.

When the ink dried, he slid the sheet into an envelope with a plain stripe. The pen lay square to the blotter; the flap pressed flat beneath his palm. Across the street, a tram rang once and was gone. The ledger balanced. That was enough.

CHAPTER 42

Rain stroked Vienna's windows with the discretion of etiquette. Carter sat by the glass, a small drink at his elbow, the envelope resting under his hand like a living thing.

Two figures crossed the park below. Wrong distance for lovers. Wrong rhythm for drunks. One tucked his chin before he looked up; the other looked fully and then tried to look casual. Carter let the curtain fall. No call to reception. No change of room. A courtesy to learners: let them chase; let them think choice was theirs.

He lifted the secure handset. Relays woke with a muted thrum.

"Sopron will hold sixteen minutes," he told his handler. "Give them a view worth the risk."

"Yes, sir."

"Nothing gratuitous," Carter added. "Just enough to make them choose again."

He hung up and smoothed the envelope. The arithmetic walked itself in his head:

Twenty-three transfers: a province keeps its lights.

Eleven: A vote cancels a flood contract.

Six: a list of names never reaches a journalist who would print without understanding.

The ledger balanced.

The light on the handset blinked once more. No operator this time; a familiar voice cut cleanly through the scramble.

"Royston. Tell me if we are solvent."

Carter's reply was as steady as his pen stroke. "We are solvent. Debts reconciled. Proof of reach established. Observers accounted for."

"Accounted for?"

"Learning," he said.

A calibrated pause carried approval better than a word.

"London tomorrow," Royston said. "Bring me the page."

"Yes."

The line thudded and fell back to its soft hum. Carter set the handset in its cradle and stood at the window again. The park lay in polite darkness; tram wires hummed their thin metallic note. He thought, briefly, of the cages—not as faces, never that—but as tonnage and timing, the solved portion of an equation.

By morning, airports would call themselves borders; ministers would name silence compassion. Carter would carry his page across a city pretending history was over, and place it on Royston's desk with ink exact, debts settled, friction tallied.

He checked the envelope's seal, pocketed it, and turned off the lamp. In the disciplined dark, solvency felt like virtue. The rain kept time.

CHAPTER 43

The freight yard at Brno lay behind them, but the train was still moving in Simon's mind — iron clatter, chains biting steel, a locked heartbeat dragging west. The tracker's pulse blinked on his monitor, steady and green, too calm for what it represented.

Julian drove without speaking. Headlights raked across stubble fields, the Lada rattling with every rut in the back road. His hand rested too firmly on the gearstick, knuckles white — a gesture Simon had learned to read. Not just stress. Control. The same ritual grip Julian used whenever the world threatened to come apart.

"They saw us," Simon said finally.

Julian didn't look over. "Of course they did."

"You mean Carter."

"I mean men like him don't miss. You don't hide from them; you just buy seconds."

The silence that followed was heavier than the engine noise. Simon tried to picture Carter's face again — that stillness, the faint lift of a cigarette ember, the look that wasn't surprise but recognition. He pushed the image aside, opened his laptop on his knees.

The feed refreshed. The container was moving faster now, coupled to a highline freight. He keyed coordinates. "Next stop's Sopron. If they don't switch lines, it'll cross into Austria before dawn."

Julian adjusted his grip on the wheel. "Austria means different eyes. Different rules."

"Safer?"

Julian gave a short, humourless laugh. "Stricter. Which isn't the same thing."

The road narrowed, pines closing in. A shadowed checkpoint loomed ahead, one lamp haloed in the mist. Simon's pulse kicked. Even derelict stations made him twitch now. Everything looked like custody.

Julian slowed, scanning. The barrier was raised, gatehouse empty. "Old post. Nobody bothers with this cut anymore."

They crossed in silence. Tyres thumped over the faded paint of a border that no longer existed. Simon kept his eyes on the tracker. The green pulse crawled, steady as breath.

Julian finally spoke. "You understand what happens if we keep following."

"I've heard your speech," Simon muttered.

"No," Julian said, colder now, deliberate. "This isn't about dogs sniffing warehouses anymore. Carter saw us. Caldwell saw us. That means we're in the file. Once you're in, you don't step back out."

Simon looked up from the screen. "Then we don't step out."

For the first time, Julian turned. His eyes were sharp even in the low light, caught between warning and a kind of reluctant admiration. His fingers tapped once on the wheel, then stilled. Ahead, the road unwound toward Austria, the night widening. The tracker blinked, relentless. Children in a steel box. A system balanced in silence. And Carter — watching.

CHAPTER 44

The town lights of Sopron shimmered on wet tarmac, amber through drizzle. Old tiled roofs sloped into the dark like hunched shoulders. Beyond them, the freight spur stretched west, floodlamps buzzing, puddles rippling with every gust of wind.

Julian killed the engine on the ridge. They sat in the rattle of cooling metal, watching.

"There." Simon pointed at the monitor. The green pulse had slowed, hovering at the coordinates. "They've held it."

Below, the container stood on a side line, chains clamped, locks squared. Men in jackets walked its perimeter. Not police, not customs — their movements were too uniform, their glances too sharp.

"Sixteen minutes," Julian murmured, watching the yard below. His tone wasn't guesswork — it was recognition. "That's not a delay. That's the window Carter would have set."

"Set for what?" Simon pressed. His eyes stayed locked on the container. "If we can get close enough, hear it, see it, anything—then we'll have proof. Not just ledgers, not whispers. Proof they can't erase."

Julian didn't answer. His gaze never left the yard.

A shunt engine rattled nearby, brakes hissing. Two trucks idled at the fence, exhaust mist blooming in the glow. A gate opened. More men stepped through. Their stance was casual, but their hands never strayed far from coat hems.

Simon's stomach twisted. "This isn't cover. It's a stage."

"Exactly." Julian's jaw was taut. "And we've been given seats."

The minutes ticked. No train moved. No lock turned. Only the handlers circling, deliberate, visible.

Simon opened his laptop, ghosting the local relay. CCTV feeds stuttered onto the screen: grainy angles of the yard, the trucks, the men pacing. No faces were clear, but the posture told enough. Disciplined. Waiting.

He whispered, "Why hold it here? Why risk being seen?"

Julian finally looked at him. "Because Carter wants to know if we'll take it. If we'll step over the line—from observers to players."

A searchlight beam swung across the siding. For a moment, it caught the container doors — steel sweating, chains taut — then swept past, grazing the ridge where they crouched. The light lingered a second too long, like a finger on glass, then moved on.

Simon's pulse hammered. "That wasn't chance."

"No," Julian said softly. His knuckles were white on the binoculars. "That was an invitation."

Below, one of the handlers tapped his watch, gestured toward the gate. Sixteen minutes. Time almost up.

The train would move again soon, and with it the cages, the children, the ledger entry sliding out of reach.

Simon's throat felt raw. "If we go in—"

Julian cut him off. "If we go in, we declare ourselves. No more shadows. No more safe distance."

The floodlamps buzzed louder, mist hissing in the air. The choice pressed down like a weight.

Sixteen minutes. One chance to matter — or walk away and let the system fold them into silence.

CHAPTER 45

The yard smelled of diesel and wet stone. Floodlamps carved hard white circles into the gravel, shadows sharp as blades.

Julian checked his watch. "Five minutes left."

Simon's throat was dry. He closed the laptop, shoved it into his pack, and forced the words out before fear could choke them back. "We go in. If we get close enough, we'll have proof. Not rumours. Not memory. Proof."

Julian's eyes narrowed. He didn't argue. He only tugged his cuff straight — the ritual gesture of composure — then pulled a hand-torch from his coat. "Quick, clean. If it goes loud, we're done."

They slid down the ridge, boots sinking into soaked earth. The chainlink fence loomed, topped with wire.

Simon dropped to one knee, pulling a field arc tool he'd built from a stripped battery pack and copper loop. A touch to the padlock. Spark, hiss, metal softening. The shackle gave with a reluctant snap.

Inside, the noise of the yard pressed closer — trucks idling, footsteps crunching, the hiss of pneumatics. They moved low, weaving through shadow. The smell of hot brake pads clung to the damp air.

The container stood ahead, steel sweating in the floodlight. Chains bit across its doors, padlocks thick and squared. Simon's gut tightened — the same design as Milan.

Julian pressed his ear to the steel, listening. At first, only wind. Then — faint, muffled. A cough. A shift of weight. A small fist thudding once, weak against the door.

Simon's breath caught. His hand shot for the lock. "We can't leave them in there."

Julian's grip clamped his wrist. "Stop. You don't know what you're opening."

"They're children."

"They're bait."

The sound came again — a scrape, then silence, as if the voices inside had learned the rhythm of the handlers' steps.

Simon's hand shook. He pulled the tracker from his pocket, but not like a gadget — like a weapon, a testimony. He pressed it hard against the undercarriage, magnets clanging to steel. The impact rang through his chest, too loud. His thumb stabbed the switch, and a green LED blinked to life. Steady. Inarguable. A heartbeat forced into the dark. Proof that could outlive both of them.

Julian hissed, "Too loud—"

A shout split the yard. Men turned, hands rising from coat hems.

"Move!" Julian snapped.

They ran low along the fence, gravel spitting underfoot. Searchlight beams slashed past, grazing Julian's shoulder, flashing sweat across Simon's cheek. Behind them, voices barked orders — not Hungarian, not Czech. English. Clipped. Professional.

They dove through the cut fence, rolled onto wet grass. The Lada waited at the ridge. Julian jammed the key, engine coughing, then catching.

In the mirror, the yard blazed with light. The container doors stayed shut, handlers reforming their perimeter. No pursuit. Just a stage resetting itself.

Simon's chest heaved. "They knew we'd come."

Julian's grip on the wheel was iron. "Of course they did. That was the lesson."

The tyres hissed over rain-slick tarmac. In Simon's lap, the tracker blinked patient, relentless — the only proof they carried.

Children in a box.

Their names already inked in Carter's ledger.

No way back.

Chapter 46

The Lada chewed at the road, engine grumbling as rain streaked the windscreen. In Simon's lap, the tracker blinked — patient, relentless — proof and curse in equal measure. Every pulse dragged them further west. Every blink said the same thing: no way back.

The road twisted through wet hills, pine dark pressing on either side. Julian drove in silence, eyes fixed on the slick tarmac, knuckles pale on the wheel. His cuff tug was sharper than usual, the tell of a man holding something back.

Finally, Simon said, "Those men in Sopron… they weren't customs. They were drilled."

Julian gave a small, cold smile. "Uniforms change. Drill never does."

Simon turned his head to the passing dark. Twice they passed abandoned checkpoints, concrete huts spray-painted with symbols: a Serbian cross with its four firesteels, crude and heavy; further on, a sunburst scrawled in red, half-washed away by rain. Even ruined, the marks looked like warnings.

"They still fight through paint," Simon muttered.

Julian's voice was quiet, but hard. "In the nineties, paint decided who lived at a roadblock. Checkerboard, eagle, lily — it didn't matter. Emblems told you whether to walk or kneel."

Simon swallowed. The thought made the green pulse on his monitor feel like another emblem — a signpost in code. Not a rescue. A test.

"They let us see them," he said.

Julian nodded once. "Because Carter wanted it. He doesn't waste risk."

"Then what are we to him?"

Julian finally looked over. His eyes were sharp even in the dark, the look of a man who had walked past too many painted walls. "We're friction. He's measuring whether we grind the gears or polish them."

Simon snapped the laptop shut, the sound loud in the car's close air. "Then we don't polish a damn thing."

Ahead, the border road straightened into black. Spray lifted under the headlights. The emblems on the ruined huts receded into the dark, but the weight of them stayed. Signs of old wars, painted over new ones.

The tracker blinked again, relentless.

Chapter 47

The Sopron yard had emptied back into silence, but the freight still dragged west in Simon's head — steel doors, chains groaning, the weight of children sealed behind them. The tracker blinked steadily in his lap, a green pulse that felt more like a heartbeat than a signal.

Now, hours later, the road had brought them to an airstrip on the Austrian side, half-shuttered, floodlights glaring through drizzle.

A Soviet-built jet sat on the apron, its nose glistening wet. Ground crew moved in tired rhythm, voices muffled under rain.

Julian slowed the Lada against the ridge. "They'll load before dawn," he said.

Simon's throat was tight. "If it's cages, we need to see them."

They left the car. The fence sagged where rust had eaten the posts; Julian pressed it down with his boot. They slid through into the dark, puddles soaking the cuffs of their trousers.

The hangar gaped open ahead, sodium lamps spilling harsh yellow light across the tarmac. Inside: rows of crates, stacked neatly, forklift idling with its hazard light pulsing. The smell of oil and wet iron clung to the air, sharp as a factory floor.

Julian crouched at the nearest crate, tracing the stencilled Cyrillic with his glove. "No customs seal. No paperwork visible."

Simon pulled his multitool — battered, Soviet steel, heavy in the hand. He worked a screw loose, heart hammering with every metallic squeak. The lid shifted, groaning open. Inside lay foam padding and black cases, narrow and long. He tilted one enough to catch the lettering: Lithium cells – hazardous.

But etched faintly on the casing, under the factory print, a falcon stooped — wings swept, talons out. Not an airline logo. Not a random flourish. A mark of ownership, precise as a signature.

Simon's chest went cold. "Not freight. This is military kit. UAV power cells."

Julian's jaw tightened. "And that mark isn't company. That's Carter's."

The forklift coughed, reversing. Shadows moved along the hangar wall. Boots struck the concrete floor, measured, steady.

Julian's hand pressed the lid closed, silent but firm. His whisper was dry as iron. "They're mixing it. Hardware in crates, children in cages. Both ledger entries."

Simon opened his mouth, fury rising — and then froze.

A voice carried through the steel echo, calm, deliberate, close enough to feel in the chest.

Carter's.

CHAPTER 48

The voice reached them before the man did—calm, unhurried, carrying clean in the hangar's echo.

"Inventory line two: reconcile and close."

Carter stepped into the light the way a surgeon steps to a table—without drama, with inevitability. Charcoal coat. Hair clipped close. A clipboard tucked under one arm like a habit. He did not glance toward the fence or the roofline. He didn't need to. Men who worked for him had already looked.

Handlers moved along the rows of crates, their pace drilled but without the theatrical snap of parade. No insignia. No chatter. A forklift idled in a steady cough, hazard lamp ticking an amber metronome across the aluminium skin of the cases. The place smelled of oil, wet concrete, jet fuel—the honest stinks that followed work. Carter preferred them to cologne and carpets.

He paused at a crate, raised the lid with two fingers. Foam. Black cases inside, long and narrow, factory labels neat: Lithium cells—hazardous. Beneath the print, faint as breath, the etched falcon showed when the light caught it. Not branding. Not flourish. A mark that said: counted.

Carter touched the edge once—no sentiment, only measure—then closed the lid. His pen moved. He wrote with the same pressure he brought to everything: even. Exact. Lines and figures that could be trusted at a minister's desk and in a back room with men who never used names.

"Audit complete," he said, without raising his voice. "No variances."

A handler repeated it for the log. It sounded like routine because it was. Routine built the world.

He walked on, ticking, initialling. He did not believe in luck. He believed in margins. In Sopron, he had held a train sixteen minutes because sixteen minutes revealed character—who would watch, who would touch, who would run. The watchers had touched; he had heard the hollow ring of a magnet kiss steel even over the yard's noise. He filed that sound beside their shadows now, where the fence sagged. One moralist. One survivor. Useful categories.

"Flight takes the first pallet at four," he told the handler who matched his stride. "No hang-ups at customs. If anyone asks, we are batteries for medical equipment."

"Yes, sir."

"Keep the page clean," Carter said. "Nothing on it I can't read aloud."

The handler nodded, then peeled away to the office where a dot-matrix rasped through carbons. Paper spoke better than men if you wrote it properly.

Carter lit a cigarette, cupped the match, and let the smoke rise into the white glare. He did not think about children. Children were not a line item you wrote; they were a pressure you balanced. The line item was solvency. Keep the lights on for the people who mattered. The rest was noise.

He stopped once more and turned his head, slow, as if considering the roof truss. He let the light take his profile

—an old courtesy to learners. He wanted them to understand: they were not unseen. They were permitted.

"Load," he said.

Chains clinked. Forks lifted. The hangar resumed its work, firm and ordinary, as though history were just freight finding the right destination.

Carter closed the clipboard. The lesson was set. He would see what they did with it.

CHAPTER 49

They didn't breathe until the forklift's cough thinned to a murmur and the boots turned away. Julian eased the crate lid back into place, two fingers on the corner to keep it from squealing, then tapped Simon once—go. They retraced their steps along the shadowed wall, slid under the fence where the wire sagged, and came up wet in the grass beyond.

The Lada's doors shut with a tired clack that sounded too loud. Julian drove without headlights for the first bend, letting the drizzle and the dark swallow them, then clicked the beams on and kept them low. The airstrip fell behind: a smear of yellow lamps and a jet's pale nose hunched in the rain.

On Simon's knees, the tracker pulsed—small, green, indifferent. Westbound. Still rail. Still moving. Proof, yes. Also an accusation.

"They're mixing it," he said, voice rough. "Cells for drones in the hangar. Children in the box. Same route. Same men."

Julian didn't answer. His hand rode the gearstick too long between shifts, a tell Simon had learned to hear even when he didn't see it. When he spoke, his tone was flat, constrained into something like calm.

"Different cargo. Same page."

"The falcon," Simon said. "That mark—"

"Don't make poetry of it." Julian's cuff tug came short and hard; he forced his hand back to the wheel. "It's a stamp that tells a certain kind of man the bill has been paid. That's all."

Simon nodded, but the image wouldn't let go: the faint etch under factory print, ownership pressed into metal like a quiet verdict. He thought of the still image from Tallinn, of Carter walking a line of cages as if counting sacks of grain. The tracker blinked again, steady as a pulse in a ward where no one called the nurse.

"We have enough to show someone," he said. "Images from the warehouse. Now the cases. The route. It's not a rumour anymore."

Julian kept his eyes on the wet ribbon of road. "Show who? The wrong person makes it disappear. The right person asks how you got it and whether you can get more. Either way, you work for them after that."

"Then we don't show. Not yet." Simon's breath fogged the window. "We keep the trail alive. Put a name next to the mark. Push until something gives."

Julian's mouth pressed thin, a shape that might have been agreement or pain. "We push Carter, he pushes back. He already has our faces. He wants to see what we are—noise or leverage."

"Then we make noise that costs," Simon said, harsher than he meant. "Children aren't a balance sheet."

Julian's jaw ticked. "To him, everything is."

They climbed into higher ground, where the road forgot it used to be a border and ran straight. In the rear-view, the airstrip's lamps dwindled to dots; ahead, the night opened into the long dark of the west.

On the tracker, the green pulse crawled on. Not dramatic. Not fast. Just undeniable.

"Vienna?" Simon asked.

"Vienna first," Julian said. "Then London. One man writes the page; the other signs it."

"Royston."

Julian didn't confirm. He didn't need to.

Rain thickened. The engine settled into its old, patient drone. Between them, in a car that smelled of damp cloth and petrol, a plan began to take the shape of a road.

CHAPTER 50

The road west unspooled in wet ribbons, the Lada's wipers beating slow time. In Simon's lap, the tracker blinked, green and patient, the only steady thing in the dark. Every pulse said the same thing: the convoy still moved. The system still held.

Neither man spoke. The hangar's smell of fuel and steel clung to their clothes, the falcon mark still etched behind Simon's eyes. When Julian finally broke the silence, his voice was tight, as though speaking risked making the truth harder.

"If they hold that pace, they'll hit Switzerland by dawn."

Simon's jaw clenched. "Then we get ahead of them. No more trailing. No more lessons."

Julian's reply was only a look — hard, appraising — before he reached into the glove box, unfolded a creased Michelin map, and spread it across the dash. His finger traced the motorway west, then stopped at a spur where the Danube narrowed into a single crossing.

"Here," he said. "One bridge. One way across. If we're faster, we get position."

Simon bent closer, heart hammering. "A view, or an intercept?"

Julian's mouth pressed thin. "You really want the second?"

Simon didn't answer. He didn't need to. The pulse in his lap answered for him.

The Lada's old engine groaned as Julian pushed it harder. Headlights carved weak tunnels through mist, spray lifting under the tyres. Frost began to ghost the verge, silvering the roadside brush. By the time they reached the bridge, the night had sharpened, brittle with cold.

Sodium lamps glowed in sickly pairs along the span, throwing long shadows into the river's black. Julian cut the headlights, eased the Lada beneath a rusting gantry, and let the engine idle down. They waited in the hush of cooling metal.

Minutes stretched. Then — engines. Heavy. Disciplined. A line of trucks appeared, headlights glaring, tyres whispering across wet steel in unison.

Simon's throat tightened. The containers rolled past in profile, locks squared, chains biting. The falcon might as well have been burned into the dark.

Julian's hand stilled on the torch. "There."

Simon followed his gaze. At the bridge's far end, a black SUV waited. Hazard lights flashed once, deliberate. Not escort. Not customs. A signal.

The convoy slowed as it passed, almost ceremonial. Last came the SUV. A window lowered just enough for the sodium glow to cut across Carter's profile. His head turned, not searching but registering. Not surprise. Recognition.

Simon's voice rasped. "We can hit the second truck. Cut the locks before they clear the span."

Julian's silence was iron.

On the tracker, the pulse blinked — proof, but also a ledger entry being inked.

Finally, Julian spoke, voice clipped. "Choice is yours. But once we cross this line, Carter writes us down."

The bridge waited.

The river carried silence below.

And the pulse went on.

Chapter 51

He hadn't raised a hand, hadn't made a move against them; they couldn't do anything. Lesson served. The convoy rolled past in measured procession, locks squared, engines steady, Carter watching from the SUV—almost mocking, as if they'd already lost. Proof still blinked green in Simon's lap, but the weight of his silence pressed heavier than iron.

An hour later, they pulled into a Rasthof. Headlights swept the slick tarmac, trucks idling in rows under the orange lamps. Inside, the café smelled of diesel, fried onions, and wet coats steaming by the heaters.

Simon dropped into a plastic chair, the cold weight of the bridge still lodged in his chest. On the counter by the till, newspapers lay damp from delivery. He pulled one free, ink smudging his fingers.

The front page showed Bosnia—refugees herded behind wire in a snowbound camp, gaunt faces jammed close, eyes hollow, breath fogging the mesh. Not Milan. Not Sopron. Yet the shape was the same: fences bending under human weight, a geometry of containment repeating itself across borders.

Julian set down two coffees, eyes flicking once to the page before sliding away. "They're selling sympathy," he said flatly.

Simon shook his head. "They're selling a version. The picture doesn't change the ledger."

By the payphones, a corkboard sagged under travel notices. Among them hung a sheet of dot-matrix print, the edges curled, tear-off slips fluttering. Courier font. Courier phrasing. alt.politics.eu.aid. The message was clipped, clinical:

EU aid → NGO fronts → manifests via Brussels. Some lines carry two ledgers.

No name, no signature. But Simon recognised the rhythm — the clause, the em dash, the clipped verb. Sophie's cadence. Not erased. Not gone.

He tore a slip free. The perforation snapped like a verdict. Coins rattled into the payphone. The receiver smelled of tobacco and bleach — same tang as the tarps in Milan. Simon clipped on the coupler, dialled an old access number. The modem sang, caught, and a header scrolled across the tiny screen:

Convoys → Brussels manifests → Liège consignments. Two cargos, one story.

Julian leaned close, reading over his shoulder. His mouth tightened. "It's her?"

"She hasn't disappeared completely," Simon said, voice low. "She's telling us where it moves next."

Julian sipped his coffee, gaze fixed beyond the glass where rain streaked the car park. "The right eyes on this and we're not ghosts anymore. We're assets."

Simon cut the line before the feed could refresh, slipped the paper into his pocket. He lifted the receiver once more, then set it back down before the beep. Some silences weren't meant to be filled.

Outside, rain smeared the windscreens. Exhaust feathered in the glow of lamps. Through Simon's jacket, the tracker blinked — steady, relentless, a pulse bound to someone else's ledger.

Julian pulled up his collar. His voice was low, final. "Liège."

"Brussels first," Simon said. "That's where both ledgers meet."

Julian gave the faintest smile, brittle at the edges. "Two ledgers. Story and truth."

They stepped back into the rain. The Rasthof lights dulled behind them, leaving only wet tarmac, truck engines, and the pulse of a system that never stopped moving west.

By dawn, it would carry them too. Toward Brussels. Toward the place where both ledgers were written.

Chapter 52

The train slid into Brussels Midi under a sky the colour of old tin. Platforms steamed with breath and cigarette smoke, the air clotted with diesel and rain trapped beneath the roof.

Simon carried the tracker deep in his satchel, its pulse steady against his ribs. Beside him, Julian walked with hands in his coat pockets, eyes always measuring reflections in the glass.

They didn't head for the Commission quarter. Too obvious. Instead, they crossed to Saint-Gilles, narrow streets thick with shuttered shops and graffiti. Aid logos stencilled on peeling posters — clasped hands, rising hearts — sagged under drizzle.

In a pay-as-you-go café wired with chipped phones, Simon clipped the coupler to the receiver and dialled the Belgian academic node. The modem squealed, then settled. Headers scrolled in courier font: clipped posts, numbers folded into phrases. Sophie's fingerprints were there again, sharp as a watermark.

NGO → relief budgets → cold chain logistics. Check Liège depots. Vans marked with pharma logos.

Julian leaned over his shoulder, eyes narrowing. "Pharma. White vans can pass anywhere."

Simon traced the posts line by line. Aid offices are bleeding funds into shell NGOs, then onto carriers registered through Gibraltar and BCCI ghost accounts. The same bank that had collapsed in scandal reappeared here in code, laundering aid through paper-thin foundations.

One invoice made him stop. Pallets listed as nutritional supplements, consignment weight doubled against the manifest. Same route: Brussels → Liège. The inversion Sophie had flagged, right there in courier strokes.

Julian tapped the line, precise, as if aligning it with memory. "Two ledgers. Aid for the cameras. The rest for Carter."

Simon leaned back, the café thick with old tobacco. Through the window, he watched a Renault van idle at the lights, pharma logo stamped clean on its flank. Steam feathered from its exhaust. Too ordinary to matter. Too precise not to.

He slid the printout across to Julian. "This isn't charity. It's cover."

Julian didn't look surprised. "Cover is Brussels' true currency."

From the street, a man raised an umbrella too late for the rain, collar high, gaze steady on the café window before he moved on. A watcher, or just reflection. Hard to tell.

Simon folded the paper into his pocket, pulse hammering. Sophie wasn't just alive in fragments. She was drawing them a map. Line by line. Ledger by ledger.

Julian drained his coffee, grimaced at the bitterness. "Next step's Liège. We see the depot. We watch the vans."

Simon nodded once, eyes fixed on the street where the van had vanished. Only the hiss of tyres on wet cobbles remained, steady as the tracker's blink in his satchel.

Brussels was noise.

Liège would be the ledger.

Chapter 53

Carter kept two ledgers.

The first was for Royston — typed neatly, ink precise, the language drained until horror looked like inventory. Humanitarian transfer. Special consignment. Debts settled. Words made safe for ministers who only skimmed margins.

The second lay open now in a pensione room off Vienna's Ringstraße. Covers cracked, paper ruled in blue, ink bleeding through thin sheets. No clerk would file it. No handler would ever admit it existed. He wrote in his own hand, black nib scratching steady as a heartbeat.

Brno – cages. Sound enough. Caldwell unsteady.

Sopron – theatre. Container displayed. Observers entered.

He paused. The nib hovered. A small pool of ink formed, dark as tar. On the next line he wrote, slowly:

They are young. Still learning.

He had never written a sentence like that before.

Carter set the pen aside and reached for the photograph folded into his wallet. He didn't open it. He didn't need to. The boy's face was already there: grin crooked, hair too long, shirt in the wrong club colours. Not alive anymore. Not for years.

He closed his eyes. The system demanded silence, not remembrance. But the picture carried its weight all the same.

From the corridor came a cough, then boots on tile. He slid the ledger into the false bottom of his case and poured himself water from the jug.

A soft knock. One of Royston's men stood in the doorway, rain dripping from his overcoat. "London expects you tomorrow. Geneva after."

"Understood." Carter shut the door before the man could speak again.

Back at the desk, he pulled the ledger free once more. Added a final line, written deliberately, each stroke slow:

Liège will prove them. Decide then.

Not "audit." Not "solvent." Those were Royston's words, tidy in green ink. This line was for himself, crooked and human, a page no one else would ever read.

He capped the pen and laid it flat. His hand lingered on the book's cover. For the first time, he was not certain which ledger told the truth — the one in Royston's files that balanced governments, or this one, where hesitation bled through ink.

Outside, tram wires hummed. A clock in the hall struck twice, chimes thin against the rain. Carter leaned back, smoke curling from the cigarette he hadn't realised he'd lit.

The arithmetic no longer reconciled. And in the space between page one and page two, something dangerous had begun to grow.

Chapter 54

The Brussels archive smelled of damp plaster and old toner. Sophie hunched over the microfiche reader, its fan whining as spools clicked past. Frames jumped and steadied, headlines surfacing in fractured light.

Kincora inquiry suspended. Allegations unproven.
Cleveland removals classed as "procedural error."
Files sealed under national security.

Her pen stabbed dots into the margin, puncturing each euphemism. Every phrase echoed what she had chased back in Cambridge — special consignment, operational mishap, humanitarian transfer. Language designed to bury meaning.

On the desk lay a printout, edges curled from travel. Simon's fragment. Manifests stripped of names, rerouted through aid fronts. Brussels consignments doubled on paper, weights that didn't balance. She underlined the inversion twice, tearing the sheet.

This wasn't Royston's invention. Men like him just stepped into a system that was already there, carrying it forward in new ink. Grooming, laundering, silencing — older than her lifetime. Older than him.

By the time the reels blurred to white, her eyes burned. She pushed back from the reader, palms damp, and stepped into the drizzle.

A café across the square glowed weakly. Inside, the air was sour with coffee grounds and wet wool. At the back, a battered terminal hummed under a striplight. She slid a floppy into the drive, keyed fast, too loud. Once, her thumb trembled on the space bar before she forced control back into her hands.

Her post was stripped to essentials:

Patterns repeat. Kincora → Cleveland → Brussels.

Always the same hand. Always green ink.

She hesitated, then added a final line:

Still here.

The screen froze. For a moment, her reflection hung, ghostly in the glass, pale and sharper than she remembered. Then the buffer cleared, and the message dissolved into the stream.

She pocketed the floppy, heart hammering, and left.

Outside, the square smelled of rain and exhaust. Two men crossed diagonally, coats dark, stride too precise for drunks or bureaucrats. One raised an umbrella, pointless against the downpour. Neither looked at her, but neither needed to. Presence was enough.

She turned down a side street, pace measured. The ghosts pressed closer — not just Kincora or Cleveland, but the children she had never seen, the cages hidden behind Simon's fragments.

Brussels called itself the capital of virtue. But Sophie had seen the second ledger, the one no committee filed and no minister admitted existed. The only question was how to force it open without being erased by it.

At the tram stop, her scarf clung wet to her throat. A white van rolled past, pharma logo glowing faintly on its flank, windows fogged from within.

She gripped the floppy in her pocket until her knuckles hurt. The ledger was never about money. It was always about children.

And she was still here.

Chapter 55

The square boiled with sound: sirens at one end, chants at the other. Antwerp's riot was neither accident nor uprising — it moved like choreography, smoke and glass breaking on cue. Flares spat against rain-slick cobbles, red light strobing off shuttered shopfronts.

Simon kept his back tight to the wall, collar turned up against the stink of petrol. Julian stood beside him, eyes scanning, each movement weighed like a soldier mapping terrain.

"Too staged," Julian muttered. "Too clean."

Through the tear gas, a line of white vans crept forward. Pharma logos bright on their flanks, paint untouched by fire. Protesters surged, screaming and waving banners — then parted without resistance each time the vans advanced. The chaos bent itself around them.

Simon crouched, dragging the laptop from his pack. The relay spat static before the signal locked. Lines of text bled onto the screen, redactions over redactions, but he saw the inversion again — the doubled weights Sophie had underlined.

"Relief supplies," he whispered. "But twice the mass. They're hiding something else inside."

Julian's jaw tightened. "Children. Or hardware. Doesn't matter. Both are leverage."

A bottle smashed near their feet, glass spraying. Ahead, one van clipped a barricade, flames licking its side. For a moment, the logo blistered. Beneath the bubbling paint, faint but deliberate, the falcon mark glimmered.

Simon's breath caught. "Carter."

A flare hissed upward, light flaring across faces — some young, painted in football scarves; others older, harder, their eyes locked not on police but on the convoy. Not a protest. A theatre. The crowd provided noise, cover, even spectacle. But the vans were the only movement that mattered.

Julian pulled him into a side street. They crouched in the mouth of the alley, smoke drifting past. The convoy rolled on, slow, steady, as if escorted by the riot rather than endangered by it. Police lines shifted just enough to open a corridor, shields angling like stage scenery.

Simon wanted to run, to wrench the locks open and show the world what lay inside. But the lesson pressed against his chest: Carter did not forbid opposition. He allowed it, measured it, and folded it back into his ledger.

The last van passed. For an instant, a handler leaned from its window, coat collar high. His gaze swept the square, lingered on the alley, and moved on without acknowledgement.

Simon flinched. Julian's grip caught his shoulder, steady, iron. "He sees us. Let him. Friction is part of the system."

Engines droned low, tyres whispering over wet cobbles. Behind them, the riot consumed itself — chants, smoke, sirens swallowed by rain. The vans receded into the east.

Simon shut the laptop with a snap. His reflection stared back from the dark screen, pale, furious. "We can't keep letting him write the story."

Julian's cufflink gleamed crooked. He didn't straighten it. "Then we wait until the story cracks."

CHAPTER 56

The riot still smouldered when they tracked the convoy east. Rain pressed smoke into the streets, leaving shards of glass and the smell of petrol clinging to their clothes.

At the edge of Antwerp, the convoy turned into a fenced depot — a yard of corrugated sheds, floodlamps harsh against wet concrete. Simon and Julian crouched behind a half-collapsed wall, watching.

Handlers moved with quiet discipline, shifting crates from trucks to vans. No shouting, no rush. Each lift had the weight of ritual, as if balance sheets were being carried in their arms. At the centre stood Carter, cigarette ember glowing, coat collar high. He gave no orders. He didn't need to.

Simon's hands shook on the laptop, trying to ghost the relay. Numbers flickered, half static, half clarity. He forced the lines into focus: Consignment 8B. Routing Brussels → Liège → Geneva. Declared cargo: lithium batteries. Adjusted weight: double. The same inversion. The same lie.

The depot gates clanged. A handler came out, folder tucked beneath his arm. For a moment, he paused — then set the folder down on a crate near the alley mouth, lit a cigarette, and walked back inside. No glance, no hesitation.

Simon's breath quickened. "It's meant for us."

Julian's eyes narrowed. "Or left to be found. Same difference."

Simon couldn't hold back. He darted from cover, snatched the folder, and slid back behind the wall. The paper was clean, typed precisely, but the weight of it pressed into his hands. The manifest was stamped with neat green ink at the bottom: humanitarian continuity.

Almost invisible in the margin, another line in a different hand: Auditors present. Let them see.

Simon looked up, eyes wide. "He knows. He wants us to carry this."

Julian's jaw flexed. "He wants us to believe that."

Across the yard, Carter drew once more on his cigarette. He didn't turn toward them. He didn't need to. His silence carried further than any command.

Engines started. Vans rolled from the depot, tyres whispering over the wet ground, falcon marks gleaming faintly beneath the logos. The gates shut with a hollow clang.

Simon clutched the folder to his chest, breath ragged. "This is proof. Not shadows. Proof."

Julian didn't answer. His gaze stayed fixed on Carter's still figure, cigarette ember fading in the rain.

Finally, he spoke, voice low, clipped. "Proof doesn't matter until it becomes a story."

Simon swallowed, the paper heavy in his hands. "Then we'll make it a story."

But even as he said it, he knew: Carter had written this page, too.

CHAPTER 57

The envelope slid across Sophie's desk with no return address. Inside: a single page, typed neatly, the ink a shade too green.

Special consignment: humanitarian continuity. Assets reconciled. Friction accounted for.

Euphemism, boiled down. A ledger dressed as mercy. She stared until the words blurred. The cadence was familiar — Royston's. His language stripped flesh into columns, silence into balance.

She set the sheet flat, uncapped her pen, and underlined each phrase once. Beneath them she wrote in her own hand:

Children. Silence. Opposition.

The words shone back at her, blunt as wounds. This was no archive relic. The system was alive now — humming in Brussels, rolling west in vans, ledger entries dressed as aid.

She scanned the page, broke it into fragments, salted it through nodes she trusted. Simon would see it. Others might too.

———

Hours later, in a hostel room thick with damp plaster, Simon unfolded the same page. Julian leaned over his shoulder.

Green ink. Phrases exact.

Julian froze. His hand hovered, then curled into a fist. "I know this."

Simon looked up. "Royston?"

Julian's eyes locked on the page, pupils blown wide, as if memory itself had clawed its way back. "Not just his hand. His voice."

The silence swelled, raw and heavy.

Julian tugged at his cufflink, frantic, breaking the ritual he always kept straight. "I was fifteen. They called it mentoring. Promising student. Access to rooms, to files. He used these words then — continuity, solvent, settled."

The chair scraped back as he stood, breath jagged. "It wasn't language. It was a leash."

Simon's chest tightened. "Julian—"

"Don't." His voice cracked sharply. "Don't tell me it was different. He wrote me into the ledger, same as the rest. Groomed. Owned. Inked into balance like a line item."

He paced, symmetry fracturing, cufflink hanging crooked. For once, he didn't fix it. His words spilt ragged: "I thought I'd escaped. Thought I was choosing my own patterns. But I was always his page."

Simon folded the memo, set it back on the table, green ink glinting faintly under the bulb. His voice was steady, though his throat burned. "Then we stop being ink. We burn the ledger."

Julian lifted his head. Eyes wet, face carved hard. For the first time, he was utterly without symmetry — raw, unshielded.

He shoved back from the table, chair scraping hard against the floorboards. His breath came fast, uneven. Brno, Caldwell, the ledger — it was all the same leash, the same ink.

"It wasn't language. It was a leash."

Simon folded the paper, hands steady even as his chest knotted. "Julian—"

Julian's voice broke sharply. "Don't. Don't tell me it was different. He wrote me into the ledger, same as the rest. Groomed. Owned. Same ink. Same lies."

He paced the narrow room, shoulders jerking, symmetry fractured. The cufflink hung loose now, crooked and gleaming.

Simon didn't try to stop him. He let the words tear loose, knowing silence could be worse.

At last, Julian sank onto the bed, head in his hands, voice raw to a whisper. "I thought I'd escaped. I thought I was choosing my own patterns. But all along, I was just another page."

Simon set the folded memo on the table, green ink shining faintly under the bulb. "Then we burn the ledger," he said.

Julian looked up, eyes wet, face hard. For the first time, there was no symmetry in him at all.

Chapter 58

The feed from Sarajevo bled into European living rooms: smoke curling from ruins, faces pressed to wire, children lifted toward cameras with hands like twigs.

In a rented flat above a Brussels print shop, Sophie leaned close to the monochrome glow of her laptop. On the desk lay her fragments: Carter's Antwerp folder, the green-ink memo, and Simon's manifests. Together, they told one story — aid convoys padded with weight that never showed in headlines.

She cut the files into pieces, salted them with plain text, then threaded them through UUCP packets. Not to ministers — they were the ledger. Not to officials — they buried the truth under seals.

She sent them east, to one name scribbled in her notebook: Peter Lynch, BBC stringer in Sarajevo.

A man who filed from ruins, not press rooms.

Her message was stripped bare:

Consignment 8B. Brussels → Liège → Geneva.

Declared: lithium batteries.

Adjusted weight: double.

Internal note: humanitarian continuity.

Private meaning: children.

Her finger hovered, pulse hammering. Then she pressed send. The buffer froze, cursor blinking like a heartbeat held. Then the packet flew. Out of her hands.

Sarajevo. Lynch crouched behind a half-collapsed wall, mic in one hand, flak jacket filthy. His satphone pinged. He scrolled through the headers, eyes widening as the phrases unfurled: Brussels depots, pharma vans, debts settled.

He looked past the wire at the camp. Mothers pushed children forward, faces hollow, voices swallowed by snow. Now he had words to cut beneath the image.

That night, his dispatch carried a caption that seared across the footage:

BBC EXCLUSIVE — EU AID MANIFESTS DOUBLE-WEIGHTED. CHILDREN VANISHED IN TRANSIT.

Governments denied. Officials deflected. But the pictures did not. Wire. Mesh. Faces pressed close. Euphemisms stripped to bone.

Back in Brussels, Sophie watched on a battered TV. Her phrases scrolled across the screen, green ink transmuted into a headline. Her chest shook. For the first time, the ledger wasn't hidden. It was public.

Across the city, in their hostel, Simon and Julian would see it too. And in whatever room he had chosen, Carter would see it — and know the story had broken loose from his columns.

Sophie pulled her scarf tight, staring at the news crawl. Her name wasn't on it. It didn't need to be. The truth had teeth now.

For Simon, the headlines were proof the world could see. For Julian, it was proof that Carter would strike back. And for Carter — ledger open, green ink bleeding into print — it was the first page he hadn't written himself.

The question now wasn't if the system would answer, but how.

Chapter 59

Whitehall smelled of polish and panic. The corridors buzzed with aides carrying folders too quickly, voices pitched too low. Doors slammed that had never been heard to slam before.

On the lobby screens, Sarajevo cages flickered: smoke, barbed wire, children pressed close. Beneath them, the BBC banner scrolled Sophie's stripped words:

DEBTS SETTLED — EU AID MANIFESTS DOUBLED

Reporters shouted questions across the barricades. Ministers avoided their eyes, retreating into black cars that gleamed under sodium light.

In his office, Royston uncapped the green pen. His hand was steady, even as the walls shook with outrage.

Consignment irregularities exaggerated. Humanitarian chain intact.

He underlined intact twice.

The phone rang before the ink dried. A voice flat and cold:

"Resignations by morning. Trade first. Then Health. You're not solvent, Malcolm."

Royston swallowed. "The ledger balances. I can show the arithmetic."

"No one's reading arithmetic anymore. They're reading headlines."

The line went dead.

He replaced the receiver with surgical care. For the first time, the green ink looked garish, childish, like paint spilt where it didn't belong.

The words he had relied on for decades — continuity, solvent, settled — bled into each other until they broke apart, leaving only the images he had sworn never to look at directly.

Brno — cages under frost.

Sopron — faces bleached by floodlights.

Antwerp — the falcon burned into steel.

Brussels — manifests that doubled weights as though doubling children.

Not inventory. Not arithmetic. Lives.

He had told himself it was language, containment, ledger work. Now the cage doors hung open in his mind and the euphemisms scattered like ash. All that remained were the children pressed to wire in Sarajevo, staring at him through a camera's lens. Staring as though they already knew his name.

For years, the arithmetic had shielded him. A balance of numbers, neat as ink. Now Carter had tipped the column. The ledger balanced without him. Worse: Carter had written him out, as coldly as he had once written debts settled.

Elsewhere, Carter sat in a Geneva hotel room, smoke curling in the glow of muted television. The same Sarajevo footage rolled, Sophie's words branded across the screen. On his lap lay the private ledger, covers cracked, notes inked in his own hand.

He slipped a page free — Consignment 8B: Brussels → Liège → Geneva — and slid it beneath the door of the journalist two rooms down.

A courtesy. A correction. A reminder that Royston had never been more than a line item.

Within hours, copies hit desks in London. The cadence was unmistakable. The handwriting damning. No one doubted.

By evening, the resignations rolled like dominoes. The Trade Minister first, voice brittle at the lectern. Then Health, eyes hollow, gaze fixed on the floor. Both denied knowledge. Both claimed regret. Neither spoke the word that burned behind the headlines.

In pubs and trains, people repeated the phrase Sophie had stripped bare. *Debts settled.* It carried now like a chant, shorthand for a truth too raw to name directly.

———

Royston sat alone as night drew down. His pen lay capped beside him, the ledger blank.

Through the window, flashbulbs flared like lightning. Each burst echoed the word that had escaped his ink, the one he had smothered for decades.

Children.

He closed his eyes, hands flat on the desk. The arithmetic could no longer protect him.

The euphemisms no longer disguised him. He himself had become an entry in Carter's book — a liability marked for erasure, a euphemism in human form.

All these years he had balanced figures, convinced it was currency. But the truth was simpler, unbearable: they had paid in children.

The silence stretched until it hardened into a verdict. He opened the bottom drawer, where the service revolver had lain untouched for decades. He weighed it carefully, like a pen in need of balance.

Outside, flashbulbs strobed. Voices clamoured. Headlines rolled without his name.

Inside, the report was short, final. A single entry, inked in gunpowder instead of green.

Royston's ledger was closed.

CHAPTER 60

The cell was square, whitewashed, and wet at the edges. A single bulb hummed overhead, throwing shadows that bent in the wrong directions.

Julian sat on the metal chair, wrists cuffed to a ring in the floor. His cufflink had been stripped from him at intake. For the first time in years, symmetry was broken.

The man across the table wore no insignia. His voice was bureaucratic, flat.

"You were seen at Sopron. At Antwerp. At the bridge. Tell us what you know of Carter."

Julian smiled, thin and tired.

"I know he keeps ledgers. Balances the books. Settles debts by trading children — and the powerful call it continuity."

The man didn't blink.

"What did he show you?"

Julian closed his eyes. Royston's green ink. The same phrases used on him years before: continuity, solvent, settled. Words that had been leash and promise both. The memory hit harder than any fist — Brno, sodium light, Caldwell's face, shame flaring like heat before he forced it down to ice.

He opened his eyes again, calm.

"He showed me how stories are written."

The man leaned closer.

"We're not interested in stories. We're interested in facts."

Julian's voice was almost gentle.

"Facts are useless unless someone believes them. That's why you're filming this. You don't want the truth. You want a version. Something you can file. Something that fits the narrative."

The guard shifted in the corner, uneasy. The interrogator's jaw twitched, just once. He pushed a folder across the table — photographs, typed notes, copies of manifests. Evidence. Ledger entries.

Julian scanned them, imprinting rhythm, cadence. The words leapt out: humanitarian continuity. Debts settled. Royston's hand again, bleeding through every page. His stomach knotted, but his face stayed smooth.

The interrogator snapped the folder shut.

"You're complicit."

Julian gave a small, crooked smile.

"No. I'm useful."

The guard's gaze lingered. Julian met it, steady, almost daring. Not a performance now, but a fragment of himself — still capable of choosing what he showed, and how.

The interrogator's eyes flicked to the camera.

"Men like you don't vanish, Julian. You're too valuable a witness — whether you agree or not."

The silence after was heavier than any threat. The interrogator studied him a moment longer, then gathered the folder.

"You'll be held. Not charged. Men like you aren't erased. You're… repurposed."

He left without another word.

Julian sat in the hum of the bulb, pulse steady. The cuffs cut into his wrists, but he barely felt them.

"I was written into a ledger once," he said softly, almost to himself. "As a boy. As property. Groomed, traded, reconciled like debt. They called it continuity."

The interrogator shifted, but Julian pressed on, voice sharpening.

"I broke. I survived. That's the only entry they couldn't balance."

Now he understood what survival meant.

Not escape. Not innocence. Narrative.

He whispered to the empty room, voice rasping against the walls:

"Truth doesn't matter unless it becomes a story."

The bulb flickered. Footsteps receded down the hall. Silence pressed close, heavy as iron. His words lingered, unfiled, unbalanced — the first line in a ledger he meant to write himself.

CHAPTER 61

The rain had followed him back across the Channel. London glistened under sodium lamps, streets slick with reflection, as if the city itself had been varnished to hide the cracks.

Simon sat in the back of the van, wrists zip-tied, laptop bag already gone. The men on either side wore plain coats, eyes steady, silence drilled.

They stopped in a cul-de-sac lined with brick terraces. No signage, no neighbours watching. One of the men opened the door, guiding him out with a hand that never quite touched.

Inside, the safehouse smelled of dust and stale carpet. A desk stood against the far wall. Behind it, a man in a navy suit with a clipped accent waited. His tie was too tight; his smile was not.

"Simon Arkwright," he said, as though testing the sound of it. "You've been busy. Milan, Sopron, Antwerp. Following convoys you weren't invited to. Picking locks you didn't own."

Simon stared at the empty chair across from him. "Charge me, then."

The man's smile thinned. "We could. Child trafficking. Espionage. Breach of the Official Secrets Act. Ten years minimum." He let the silence settle, heavy. Then: "Or—"

Simon lifted his chin. "Or what?"

"Or you work for us. MI6 needs hands like yours. Fingers that know locks. Eyes that see patterns." He slid a folder across the desk. Inside: photographs of Simon in Sopron, on the bridge, crouched in the rain beside Julian. Every angle precise.

"You were flagged long before Cambridge," the man said softly. "Cambridge only confirmed what we already knew. We just had to wait until you fell into the right column."

Simon's stomach turned. His life hadn't been chance or choice. He had been in their files since Belfast, carried forward like unfinished business.

"Prison or service," the man said. "You know which keeps you useful."

Simon's pulse hammered. He wanted to spit refusal, to burn every bridge. But the folder lay open, his own face grainy under surveillance light. His name already marked.

Slowly, he sat. The chair's legs scraped the floor, loud as a verdict.

"I'm not your man," he said. "I'm your tool. Tools break."

The man's smile returned, faint and satisfied. "Tools can also cut."

The zip-ties were snipped. A contract lay waiting, not legal, not optional. Simon didn't pick up the pen. He only stared at it, fury tight in his chest.

He was no longer free. He was an asset.

Chapter 62

The committee chamber was airless, wood-panelled, built to smother heat. Rows of microphones blinked red. Reporters filled the back benches, pens twitching like weapons.

Sophie stood at the table, the folder heavy in her hands. Carter's page, Royston's memo, Antwerp's manifest — every fragment gathered and aligned. Proof cut into shape.

A minister leaned forward, voice smooth as varnish.

"Ms Patel, we have reviewed your submissions. Aid convoys are complex. Errors inevitable. Are you suggesting malice?"

Sophie met his gaze.

"I'm suggesting intent."

A murmur rippled through the room. She laid the papers flat, palm pressed to steady them.

"Brussels declared lithium batteries. Geneva reconciled tonnage. The weights never matched. NGO fronts masked transit. Green-ink phrases told officials what they wanted to believe: humanitarian continuity. Debts settled. The language of a ledger, not relief."

She lifted one page — Royston's memo, the green ink glistening under the lights.

"This was the script. Precise. Deliberate. But not truthful."

She held it higher, voice stripped of inflexion.

"They weren't just trafficked. They were tallied. Balanced like numbers. Settling accounts when money left too clear a trail. Children were currency."

The room had no answer. Euphemisms dissolved into what they had always meant.

She set the paper down and spoke louder, each word a blade.

"This ledger only worked because lives were treated as entries — bought, traded, erased. Every phrase was arithmetic masking atrocity."

The chamber froze. No pen scratched. No cough broke the air. One reporter dropped his notebook, the thud loud against the hush.

The minister opened his mouth, closed it again. His hand fumbled with the papers, as if they might rearrange themselves into something safer.

Sophie kept going, voice steady.

"Special consignment. Continuity. Settled debts. Every euphemism was a line in the book. Every silence a zero that let the column balance. This was not an error. This was design."

She pushed the folder toward the clerks.

"You wanted arithmetic. Here it is. Every number reconciles. Every phrase decoded. Look at it. Then decide if you still want to call this humanitarian."

Flashes burst from the back benches. Reporters leaned forward, hungry. The words were already leaving the room, already writing themselves into tomorrow's front pages.

Sophie drew in a slow breath. She had carried ghosts from Kincora, from Cleveland, from Brussels. Now they stood in daylight, ledger ink stripped of camouflage.

She gathered her scarf around her neck and said the last line for herself, not the chamber:

"Don't disappear completely."

The microphones hummed on. The ledger was open, and this time, the world was reading it.

CHAPTER 63

The Geneva hotel room was empty by the time the handlers arrived. The wardrobe hung open, hangers bare. The bedspread was smooth, no crease where a body had lain.

On the desk sat a single ledger, bound in cheap board. Not Royston's pages, not the green ink. Carter's own hand.

The first leaves were filled in steady script — consignments, routes, ministers briefed, opposition observed. Then the entries thinned, margins wide, words fewer.

On the final page, written larger than the rest, stood one line:

Opposition is proof that the system works.

No signature. Just the sentence, ink pressed so hard it bled through the paper.

The handlers searched anyway. Drawers, bathroom, window frame. Nothing. Passport gone, case gone, the man himself gone.

A cigarette smouldered in the ashtray, filter crushed flat. Still warm.

By evening, the ledger reached London. Royston was already finished, name rotting in headlines. The ministers who remained argued whether Carter's note was a confession or defiance. Some said he had fled east. Others whispered he had been silenced.

But the ledger itself carried no trail. Just the phrase, immovable, as if written for whoever next picked up the pen.

Simon read the photocopy in a safehouse outside Cambridge. The words sat heavy on the page, harder than iron.

BOOKS BY THIS AUTHOR

Before The Shadows Rise

★★★★★ "Smart, human, and chillingly plausible… hooked from the first page." — Verified UK Reader

★★★★★ "A must-read for action and thriller fans alike… gripping and authentic." — Amazon UK Reviewer

Belfast, 1994. A civilian girl dies during an SAS mission. The official story calls it justified. Adam Hayes knows it wasn't. He wasn't the shooter—but he was there. And silence has haunted him ever since.

Decades later, in the jungles of Belize, Hayes and fellow operative Tony Shaw uncover a trail linking cartel weapons, Cold War black sites, and a manuscript whispered about in intelligence files: Visiones Stellarum.

At the centre is The Horsemen—a ruthless network hidden in plain sight, leaving symbols in warzones and bodies in their wake. Every clue exposes another cover-up. Every step forward brings assassins, betrayals, and echoes of the one mistake Hayes never outran.

Now, hunted across continents, Hayes must choose: stay silent and survive—or face the truth, and bring down the enemy who has been rewriting history for decades.

Before the Shadows Rise is a relentless blend of covert warfare, dark conspiracy, and one man's fight for redemption"

The Horsemen's Shadow

★★★★★ "Nothing short of extraordinary — a cinematic, pulse-pounding thriller that fuses ancient prophecy with bleeding-edge science." — Sarah, Verified Purchase

★★★★★ "A potential bestselling thriller for 2025/26 from J.N. Paul, a new master of the genre."

Every disaster was planned. The next one is already here. Wars. Pandemics. Financial crashes. They weren't random. They were engineered. And the truth is about to be exposed. The Chase Begins

When an encrypted file surfaces, three unlikely allies are pulled into a deadly conspiracy thriller across the globe: An ex-SAS soldier haunted by his past, A CIA whistleblower with a target on his back an academic guarding a secret the Vatican tried to bury.

The Discovery: Visions of the Stars — a Vatican manuscript linking ancient prophecy, planetary alignments, and a modern blueprint for collapse. A secret society has been scripting history for centuries. Their final move has already begun: Phase Zero. What to Expect: From hidden vaults in Rome to black-ops raids and satellite warfare, this is a fast-paced, action-adventure that will grip fans of Dan Brown, James Rollins, and Robert Ludlum.

The Horsemen are riding. And billions of lives are on the line.

Printed in Dunstable, United Kingdom

68323552R00137